Ducky

California Diaries #5

Ducky

Ann M. Martin

SCHOLASTIC INC.
New York Toronto London Auckland Sydney

*The author gratefully acknowledges
Peter Lerangis
for his help in
preparing this manuscript.*

ISBN 0-590-29839-9

12 11 10 9 8 7 6 5 4 3 2 1   8 9/9 0 1/0 2/0

Printed in the U.S.A   40

First Scholastic printing, February 1998

Saturday is Valentine's Day.

So we will be allowed to celebrate it at school TOMORROW, Friday.

Unless you don't have a Valentine. Like me.

Then you don't celebrate. You walk around feeling sorry for yourself. You might as well stay home.

But look on the bright side, McCrae.

Tomorrow ALSO happens to be Friday the 13th.

So maybe having a Valentine is unlucky. And the best thing to do is go to school and don't worry.

You will not worry.

You will not worry.

You will not worry.

During Homeroom, F the 13
Tucked into a Looseleaf Notebook

The place is a zoo, and it's all my fault.

Flowers everywhere. Teachers acting like kids. Jason tongue-wrestling with Lisa out in the hallway.

JAY, not JASON.

JAY.

JAY.

I HATE THIS. YOU KNOW SOMEBODY FOR YEARS — HE'S SPENT A WHOLE LIFETIME WITH ONE NAME, AND ALL OF A SUDDEN BOOM HE DECIDES ANOTHER ONE IS COOLER. SO NOW YOU HAVE TO THINK EVERY TIME YOU SEE HIM, AND THEN YOU HAVE TO CALL HIM A NAME THAT DOESN'T FIT, SORT OF LIKE CALLING A TELEPHONE A TOASTER — BUT GOD FORBID YOU DON'T, BECAUSE HE'LL GET MAD AT YOU, AND OF COURSE IT WOULD NEVER OCCUR TO HIM OR ANYONE ELSE TO WONDER IF YOU MIND BEING CALLED "DUCKY," A NAME YOU DIDN'T CHOOSE, BECAUSE YOU'VE ALWAYS BEEN KNOWN BY IT AND BESIDES, IT'S BETTER THAN THE NAME THE CRO MAGS USED TO CALL YOU, "BAMBI" — AND HEY, CRO MAG IS A NICKNAME YOU THROW AROUND, BUT THAT'S JUST A DESCRIPTION, BECAUSE THOSE MUSCLE-HEAD JOCKS DO ACT LIKE PREHISTORIC CRO-MAGNON CAVEPEOPLE — PLUS, WHEN YOU THINK ABOUT IT, "DUCKY" FITS ANYWAY BECAUSE IT'S WEIRD AND FUNNY AND SO ARE YOU.

ANYWAY, CONGRATS, McCRAE. YOU DID V DAY RIGHT THIS YEAR. YOU DID NOT:

... STAY HOME AND HIDE, LIKE YOU WANTED TO.

... LET BIG BROTHER TED TALK YOU INTO A BLIND DATE, LIKE THE ONE TWO YEARS AGO WITH SHELAIGH, WHO WORE MORE MAKEUP THAN CLOTHING AND WHOSE GREATEST TALENT WAS ROLLING HER EYES, TAPPING HER FEET, AND LOOKING AT HER WATCH IN THREE DIFFERENT RHYTHMS.

... WRITE EVERY SINGLE GIRL IN YOUR CLASS A POETIC LOVE NOTE, LIKE YOU DID IN SEVENTH GRADE, CAUSING MANY OF THEM TO GANG UP

AGAINST YOU ON THE PLAYGROUND AND THREE PARENTS TO CALL MOM &
DAD COMPLAINING YOU'D BROKEN THEIR DAUGHTERS' HEARTS.

...MAKE MOM A VALENTINE'S DAY CARD WITH SO MUCH GLUE
THAT IT STUCK TO THE KITCHEN TABLE AND SHE GOT MAD AT YOU SO
YOU FLUSHED THE CHOCOLATES YOU WERE GOING TO GIVE HER DOWN THE
TOILET AND CLOGGED IT UP, RUINING THE WHOLE DAY FOR EVERYONE...
THAT WAS FOURTH GRADE, I THINK.

NOPE, DUCKY OLD BOY, YOU'VE LEARNED THE HARD WAY. YOU
DON'T NEED A SPECIAL SOMEONE. TODAY YOU WERE EVERYONE ELSE'S
SPECIAL SOMEONE.

WITH STYLE.

THE FAKE HALO MADE OF TWIST-TIES, THE BOW AND ARROW SLUNG
OVER YOUR BACK, THE BIG BASKET OF CARNATIONS — BRILLIANT. ALL
THAT WAS MISSING WAS A MARQUEE OUT FRONT — "CHRISTOPHER
'DUCKY' MCCRAE IS CUPID!"

THE GIRLS LOVED IT. ESPECIALLY SUNNY, WHO PLANTED A BIG
WET ONE ON YOUR LIPS, THEN ACTUALLY THREADED THE STEM OF THE
CARNATION THROUGH HER NAVEL RING AND FLASHED IT AROUND, UNTIL
MR. DEAN CAME OUT OF THE OFFICE. DAWN PUT HER FLOWER IN HER
LONG BLONDE HAIR AND SPUN AROUND, DOING SOME FOLK-DANCEY THING
THAT MADE HER PEASANT DRESS SPIN OUT. MAGGIE KISSED HERS AND
SAID SHE WOULD WRITE A SONG ABOUT IT.

GIVING FLOWERS TO THE TEACHERS — THAT WAS THE BEST IDEA
OF ALL. FROM THE LOOK ON MS. PATTERSON'S FACE, EXPECT AN A IN
MATH THIS SEMESTER.

OKAY, SO NOT EVERYONE WAS AMUSED. MR. DEAN COULDN'T

DECIDE WHETHER TO THROW YOU OUT OR LAUGH. AND ALEX SORT OF LOOKED RIGHT THROUGH YOU (THAT THOUSAND-YARD STARE OF ALEX SNYDER). AND THE CRO MAGS, OF COURSE, HAD A FIELD DAY, GRUNTING AND SCRATCHING AND PASSING NASTY COMMENTS TO EACH OTHER. YOU HAVE TO TAKE THE GOOD WITH THE BAD.

BUT HERE'S ANOTHER BIG CHANGE. A YEAR AGO, McCRAE, THE CRO MAG COMMENTS WOULD HAVE KILLED YOU. A YEAR AGO, YOU WORRIED ABOUT THEIR OPINIONS. YOU WANTED THEM TO BE YOUR FRIENDS. HOW MANY YEARS DID IT TAKE TO REALIZE THEY WERE GOING TO MAKE FUN OF YOU NO MATTER HOW HARD YOU TRIED TO BE LIKE THEM?

AS IF YOU EVER COULD.

SO... IF YOU CAN'T JOIN THEM, DO EXACTLY WHAT THEY HATE. LIKE DANCE PAST THEM, SINGING "ALL YOU NEED IS LOVE," AND TOSS THEM A FLOWER — THEN WATCH THE LOOK ON MARCO BARDWELL'S FACE THE MOMENT AFTER HE CATCHES IT AND REALIZES HIS APELIKE FRIENDS ARE NEVER GOING TO LET HIM LIVE IT DOWN.

DUCKY, YOU MAY BE STRANGE BUT YOU ARE A GENIUS.

IF ONLY ~~JASON~~ JAY HADN'T GOTTEN SO BENT OUT OF SHAPE. JAY, BEING ONE OF YOUR OLDEST FRIENDS, SHOULD KNOW YOUR SENSE OF HUMOR, BUT OBVIOUSLY HE DOESN'T, BECAUSE HE ACTED LIKE YOU HANDED HIM A DEAD SQUID AND MUTTERED, "DO YOU ALWAYS HAVE TO MAKE A FOOL OF YOURSELF?"

DO YOU?

DO I?

Even Later That Afternoon
In Math Class, to Be Exact

1.

1.

1.

Why do I call myself "you" all the time? This can't be normal. Only I don't know, because to figure out what "normal" is, I'd have to read other people's journals and I'm not allowed because Vista requires you to keep yours PRIVATE, to "provide you with a personal learning experience," but it WOULD be nice if you could at least see A LITTLE of someone else's, because soon the world will be full of Vista students with piles of unread journals and that seems like such a waste of both paper and interesting stories.

What it boils down to is this: Writing "I" is creepy. TOO PERSONAL. You feel self-conscious. You worry about how you come across. But with "you," it's like you're another person. It's just easier, that's all. It's easier to be someone else.

Here comes Ms. Patterson. If she sees this, I'm toast.

2B cont.

Home at Last
Still Depressed
But Not Toast

I wish I hadn't written that.

The part about being someone else.

I've been thinking about it all day.

It's kind of pathetic, in a way. Like you can't stand being yourself.

I asked Sunny about this. I asked her if she ever wanted to be someone else.

She said she always wants to be someone else.

Which is RIDICULOUS because she's great exactly the way she is (I told her so), but she just said that if I were in her shoes — if MY mom had cancer, if MY dad spent all his time at the hospital and at his bookstore — I'd be pretty upset too.

I shouldn't have opened my big mouth. I shouldn't have used the word ridiculous. I know the pressure she's under. I'm the one who found her that night at Venice Beach, alone and scared, dumped by that guy she wanted to run away with. OF COURSE she thinks about being someone else. Her life is no picnic and I WOULDN'T want to be in her shoes.

But the thing is, even though I'm NOT in her shoes I STILL feel depressed.

This is a DEEP-INSIDE problem, not a BAD CIRCUMSTANCES problem.

At least Sunny KNOWS who she is. You can tell by looking at her — the weird hair, the funky layered outfits, the body piercings or magnetic studs or whatever those things are. Even her opinions — loud and clear even when they're wrong — all of it says THIS IS ME, SUNNY WINSLOW, TOO BAD IF YOU DON'T LIKE IT.

Dawn's like that too. She can obsess a LITTLE about the environment and global warming and health foods and yada yada, but you always know where she stands.

And Maggie. Serious, intense, attitude-of-the-month Maggie. Committed punk rebel for awhile, preppy good girl until that wore off, star rock singer after that. Always changing but STRONG, never really DRIFTING.

Amalia Vargas is another one. Sharp, full of opinions, and so COMMITTED to her artwork.

They don't seem three years younger. They're such personalities. Definite, clear personalities.

I wish I felt like that. I never know how to BE.

I know how NOT to be. NOT prep. NOT grunge. NOT jock. NOT high-tech nerd.

Step right up, folks — meet Ducky McCrae, Palo City's number one NOT! Make your own guess about what he is. EVERYBODY else has an opinion. Choose from the options below:

A. Sissy wimp girlie man — the Cro Mag perspective, shared by a certain species of Vista School male.

B. Immature stupid little kid — Ted and friends.

C. Oddball child — Hi, Mom and Dad, wherever you are.

D. Carefree, mature, laugh riot — Sunny and friends.

E. Not.

Personally I love D., but it's just as wrong as A.-C.

SO... WHAT AM I?

Defining Ducky
A Madcap Confessional Romp
REEL ONE, TAKE ONE

[Enter Ducky McCrae, a nondescript 16-year-old with a few pimples and nondescript brown hair, wearing nondescript pants and shirt bought from a vintage clothing store. He looks in mirror and sees... nothing.]

DUCKY: I am... a 16-year-old who hangs out with 13-year-olds.

"Robbing the cradle." That's what Jay called my friendships with Sunny & Co. I didn't know what it meant, until Ted explained: It's how you describe someone who's going out with someone else much younger — which is typical of the way Jay's mind works, imagining that I'm dating those girls all at the same time... and that they don't mind. Which not only is wrong but insulting to Sunny, Maggie, Amalia, and Dawn, because they're way too smart and independent to let themselves be treated like that. And besides, now that Jay is going Cro Mag on me — and Alex is just fading away and has hardly said two

WORDS TO ME SINCE NEW YEAR'S — THOSE THREE GIRLS ARE BECOMING MY CLOSEST FRIENDS. THIRTEEN OR NOT. AND THAT'S THAT.

DUCKY: I AM...A VIRTUAL ORPHAN.

THAT IS EXACTLY THE WAY I FEEL. DUCKY AND TED'S EXCELLENT ORPHAN ADVENTURE. NO PARENTS, NO RULES. SEE THE DECORATIVE PILES OF LAUNDRY IN EVERY ROOM, GATHERING DUST. ADMIRE THE FOOD ON THE WALLS AND FLOORS, THE DISH SCULPTURE IN THE SINK. THE 23 HALF-FULL BOXES OF CEREAL. THE REFRIGERATOR FULL OF SODA, ICE CREAM, AND A CARROT LEFT OVER FROM LAST YEAR. ENOUGH TO HORRIFY ANY ADULT, EXCEPT TECHNICALLY TED IS AN ADULT, WHICH IS A LAUGH, BUT SOMEHOW HIS 20-YEAR-OLDNESS MAKES IT LEGAL FOR MOM & DAD TO SPEND MONTHS IN GHANA WHILE THEIR SONS EAT TAKE-OUT PIZZA AFTER OCCASIONAL PATHETIC ATTEMPTS AT COOKING DINNER.

I MEAN, COME ON. WHOSE PARENTS GO ON EXTENDED BUSINESS TRIPS TO GHANA? OR TO QATAR, OR ABU DHABI, OR SRI LANKA? CAN YOU POSSIBLY GET FARTHER AWAY FROM YOUR CHILDREN?

ENOUGH ABOUT THAT. BACK TO THE SCREENPLAY.

DUCKY [STILL LOOKING IN MIRROR]: I AM...EVERYBODY'S BEST FRIEND.

ACCORDING TO SUNNY, AT LEAST.

AND MAYBE IT USED TO BE TRUE. I STILL HAVE THE JOURNAL

FROM 6TH GRADE, WHERE I COUNTED MY FRIENDS AND CAME UP WITH 47.

Not anymore, though. Not since the Cro Mags started ganging up on me in 8th grade. And Jason became JAY. And Alex became

What HAS Alex become?

When I gave him that flower this morning — nothing. No laugh, no wisecrack, no response at all. As if this kind of scene happened every day and he was bored with it.

Alex the Morph.

This is NOT the Alex I grew up with. It's as if some alien ship came down and sucked out his soul.

I stared at him today at lunch, while he wasn't looking. The same way I used to when we were kids and I'd try to send an ESP message, and most of the time he'd notice I was staring and sometimes he'd even GET the message. And we were convinced we could read each other's minds, because we always finished each other's sentences and we liked the same movies and books and CDs and TV shows, and we could look at each other — just look — and both burst out laughing. No one knew why, but WE did, because we'd both be thinking of EXACTLY THE SAME THING. And sometimes at home I'd reach for the phone to call him, and the phone would immediately ring, and it would be him. And we'd talk and talk until Mom would get angry and I'd look at the clock and see that TWO HOURS had gone by and it felt like two minutes.

And that person is gone gone gone, lost somewhere between 9th and 10th grade, replaced by a total stranger who doesn't know I'm alive.

I keep saying to myself, hey, it's because his parents divorced. But that happened so long ago, and he did seem to bounce back. What's going on now?

I wish he'd tell me. He doesn't seem to actually HATE me or anything. He lets me sit with him during lunch. No one else seems to want to sit with him these days — least of all JAY.

He's decided that Alex has totally dropped off the coolness radar or something.

I thought I had dropped off it too, after this morning. But maybe not. JAY finally apologized to me. I guess when you're such a jerk so often you learn how to say "I'm sorry." JAY has always been so good at that. And face it, McCrae, you are such a SUCKER for a good apology. They can hit you over the head, strip you naked, cut off your legs, and gouge out your eyes, but as long as they say, "Sorry about that, man," you forgive them.

Anyway, JAY was arm in arm with Lisa Bergonzi, who was wearing the wilted carnation behind her left ear. And he said something like, "Yo, Duckster, remember that flower? And what I said and all, about you making a fool of yourself? I didn't mean to say it. It was just ... you know ..."

Dot dot dot. What? I just looked at him, waiting for him

TO GO ON, BUT ALL HE SAID WAS, "I GAVE IT TO LISA, OKAY? SHE REALLY LOVED IT."

LISA SMILED AND THANKED ME.

JAY WAS LOOKING AT ME EXPECTANTLY. I FELT LIKE I HAD TO GIVE MY APPROVAL OR SOMETHING. SO I SAID, "GREAT."

LISA LEANED HER HEAD ON HIS SHOULDER. HE TURNED AND HUGGED HER, LIFTING HER OFF HER FEET. THEN THEY WALKED AWAY, MAKING OUT. AND I MEAN DEEP-KISSING. WITH THEIR EYES CLOSED. WHILE WALKING. I WAS SURE THEY WOULD CRASH INTO THE GLASS DOOR, BUT THEY DIDN'T.

MUST BE SOME KIND OF TECHNIQUE. I WOULDN'T KNOW.

I SHOULD KNOW. IT IS TOTALLY WEIRD TO BE 16 AND NEVER KISSED LIKE THAT.

IT IS TOTALLY WEIRD TO HANG OUT WITH 13-YEAR-OLDS.

IT IS TOTALLY WEIRD TO LIVE ALONE IN A BIG HOUSE WITH YOUR BROTHER AND YOUR COMBINED FILTH.

ISN'T IT?

MAYBE THAT'S THE ANSWER TO "WHAT AM I?"

TOTALLY WEIRD.

[SKIES DARKEN. THE MIRROR BECOMES BLUISH. DUCKY'S FACE SINKS. HE LOOKS HIMSELF IN THE EYES.]

DUCKY: BUT REALLY, I DON'T KNOW WHAT I AM.

Feb. 13
I Don't Even Want to Look at the Clock

I HATE THIS JOURNAL.

WHO WAS MS. NEWELL TRYING TO KID BACK IN 8TH GRADE WHEN SHE SAID JOURNAL WRITING WAS GOOD THERAPY?

IT'S NOT.

I FEEL WORSE THAN EVER.

LAST ENTRY.
END OF JOURNAL.

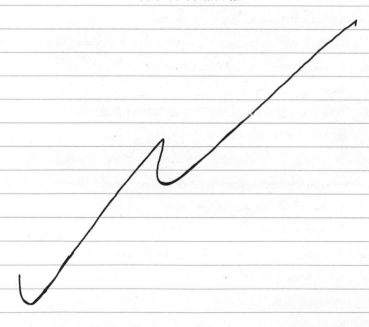

Feb. 14, Sat. Morning
I Lied

Two phone calls today. Your social calendar is just filling up, McCrae.

Sunny wants to go to the beach. Actually, she demanded you drive her (and Maggie and Dawn).

And...

JAY called.

He wants to talk. He STILL feels bad about what he said yesterday morning. Even after his "apology," he thinks you're mad at him. (I WONDER where he gets THAT idea?) So you're supposed to meet him at the Palo City Diner at 6.

You said you'd get back to him.

What if it's a trick? What if he plans to bring along a gang of Cro Mags? He's VERY tight with them.

Would he do that?

People don't change THAT much, do they?

Whoa. Ease up.

You know, McCrae, you are one harsh creature. He DID apologize. He is reaching out to you.

He is TRYING to be friends again.

You scribble away in your journal, trashing one of your best friends, calling him a Cro Mag, making fun of him when he tries to say he's sorry, and what's he doing?

Planning ways to make you feel better.

So Jay's crude. Big deal. You've always known that about him. BUT he's always had that big heart too. Imagine if he hadn't stood up for you back in 7th grade when Sal Mignona was beating you to a pulp. You'd be dead by now.

Face it. He hasn't really changed. He's the same guy you used to like. So what if he's discovered girls. And hair gel. And cologne. And free weights.

He'll get over it.

Thought of the day: Jay is the opposite of Alex. One has faded. The other has intensified.

De-Alexation. Ultra-Jasification.

Too bad they can't rub off on each other.

Anyway, you have to stay friends with both of them. It's not like the whole sophomore class is breaking down your door to be friends.

So call Jay back. Tell him you'll meet him at the diner.

Besides, consider the alternative. Ted brought home a can of Spam and a loaf of day-old Wonder Bread for dinner.

It's a no-brainer.

Sur La Plage

DUCKY YOU ARE SO PRETENSUOUS!
LOVE, SUNNY

I think the word is "pretentious."

IT TAKES 1 TO KNOW 1, MAGGIE.

It's just French. Okay, here, in English:

At the Beach

Are you happy now?

Dawn wuz here

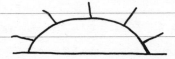

That's a sunset!

DEPENDS ON THE WAY YOU LOOK AT IT!

You girls are wild.

Please keep your suntan oil OFF the page. And your fruit juice!

I should NOT have brought this <u>PRIVATE!</u> journal to the beach!

I GET NO RESPECT.

NEITHER DO I!

Home Alone Again

I guess Ted ate the Spam. It's gone and so is he.

Too bad. I'm hungry.

I did not eat a thing at the diner. I was too shocked by Jay's STUPID stunt!

I knew I shouldn't have gone. I had a bad feeling about it.

I had the BEST time at the beach AND I NEVER SHOULD HAVE LEFT!

What kind of "friend" invites you to dinner, making you think you're going to have a 1-on-1 talk, and then shows up with 2 extra people to make it suddenly 1 on 3, but they're both girls, 1 of which is Lisa and the other is all dressed up and made up, so it dawns on you (DUH) that it's really supposed to be 2 on 2 and you've been trapped in a blind double date and now there's no way out?

WHAT KIND OF SNEAKY JERK OF A FRIEND WOULD DO THAT?

The Friend Formerly Known as Jason, that's who.

And he doesn't have the decency to let you KNOW IN ADVANCE, so you don't feel AMBUSHED!

Emergency. Fight or flight. THAT'S how you feel. And you can't do either one. You just have to sit there and smile and laugh and nod and wish you were home with Ted and the Spam because anything would be better than this, and Jay is running

HIS FINGERS THROUGH HIS GELLED HAIR ALL NIGHT AS IF HE WERE PLOWING A CROP, WHILE HE TALKS AND TALKS AND TALKS AND TALKS ABOUT — WHAT ELSE? — HIMSELF.

UNTIL HE GETS AROUND TO TALKING ABOUT YOU AND SAYING WHAT A GREAT GUY THE DUCKSTER IS, REALLY, A NATURAL ATHLETE WHO DOESN'T EVEN KNOW HIS OWN STRENGTH, NOT TO MENTION A REAL BRAIN TOO, DON'T BE FOOLED BY THE WIMPY HAIRCUT AND HAWAIIAN SHIRT HAR-HAR.

YOU WANTED TO KILL HIM.

WHAT COULD YOU SAY? HE WOULDN'T STOP TALKING. YOU TOLD A FEW DUMB JOKES. SOME STUFF ABOUT SOFTWARE AND TV COMMERCIALS AND WHATEVER, AND YOU COULD TELL YOU SOUNDED LIKE A TOTAL FOOL BECAUSE THE GIRL WAS JUST STARING AT YOU, HER SMILE TIGHTENING BY THE SECOND, AND YOU KNOW SHE WAS THINKING, "HOW DID I GET ROPED INTO A DATE WITH THIS TURKEY?" AND AFTERWARD YOU HAD TO DRIVE HER HOME BECAUSE JAY HINTED LOUDLY THAT HE AND LISA WERE GOING OFF IN A DIFFERENT DIRECTION, SO SHE AND YOU RODE SILENTLY TO HER HOUSE AND YOU COULD TELL SHE COULDN'T WAIT TO GET OUT OF THE CAR AND YOU DON'T EVEN REMEMBER HER NAME!

I WILL KILL HIM.

Feb. 15
The Morning After
The Night Before

How could he do it?

I can't figure it out.

A day later, a whole night's sleep, and I'm supposed to be calmer and more rational but my teeth are still gritted so hard I haven't tried eating breakfast and I'm not hungry anyway because I AM STILL FURIOUS.

Did he think I'd LIKE to be surprised like that? Is he that stupid?

Or was I wrong about him? Has he REALLY gone Cro Mag on me? Maybe the other goons were watching the whole scene behind the jukebox. Taking pictures. Videotaping. "The Humiliation of Ducky, as choreographed by Jay Adams." Order your copies now, folks!

Or is it ME? Maybe this is NORMAL. Maybe guys DO this kind of thing for other guys.

Maybe you're supposed to like it.

So now what?

Are you supposed to call the girl and ask her on another date? Hold hands in the hallway and walk to classes together and save seats for each other at the lunch table?

How can you do ANY of that when you can barely remember what she looks like and what you REALLY need to do is talk to your traitor-friend and ask him WHAT IS IN HIS TWISTED MIND. Which you can't even do because your fingers get to 555-837 and then — FREEZE — you feel all tongue-tied. What can you SAY when your mind is so full of anger you want to scream and you're afraid that's just what you'll do, which will cause your ex-best friend to hang up and never hear your side of the story at all?

You put down the phone and leave, that's what.

You spend some time alone.

Part 2 of the Continuing Saga:
How Not to Choose Your Friends

What you do is, you fly through town on your bike to Las Palmas County Park and hit the trail so fast you nearly run over a hiker who calls you nasty names and makes you feel even worse, if that's possible. So you slow down and you remember the place where you used to hide when you were a kid and you needed to be alone, the place hidden in the reeds by the bank of the creek near the old bridge. And you smile, remembering the summer days you and Alex used to spend there — just talking — and as you're gliding across that bridge you see a mass of black pants and a flannel shirt hiding in the same spot and you tense up, figuring you're going to be sneak-attacked by a

Cro Mag, or maybe he's strung fishing wire across the bridge at neck level — and the pants and shirt turn out to be Alex.

So you skid to a stop, jump off the bike, and walk around the bridge. And you have a conversation that goes something like this:

Ducky: "Hey, Alex!" [Pause, pause, pause ...] "Uh, Alex, hi! What's up?"

Alex: [Looks up. Expression hardly changes.] "Oh. Yo. Nothing much."

D: "Waiting for somebody?"

A: "Nahh."

D: "Just, like, sitting?"

A: "Yup."

D: "Wow. Just like the old days, huh?" [Pause, pause, pause.] "Well, nice day for sitting."

A: [Nods. Pulls grass from the ground and tosses it aside.]

D: "Are you okay?"

A: "Yup."

D: "Okay, well, 'bye." [Walks away.]

A: "Hey. Ducky. That Valentine's Day flower? That was cool."

D: "Yeah?"

A: "Nicest thing anyone's given me in months."

BONNNNG, rings a bell in the cuckoo clock of your brain. And out comes a little bird that says, "Déjà vu. Déjà vu. Déjà vu."

Here's where you see, for the first time on this stage in many a year, folks, the Person That Was Once Alex.

Because you knew — somehow YOU JUST KNEW — that he was going to say that. And maybe you just knew he'd be near the bridge. And you haven't had those ESP-ish feelings in a million years.

But you're not exactly sure how to take what he said. THE nicest thing? Your stupid little Cupid carnation that you gave to everybody? He must be joking. In which case it's the first hint of humor you've heard from the New Alex.

But he's not smiling. The expression on his face is very Old Alex, and it tells you he's speaking the truth.

And that's about the saddest thing you've heard all day.

D: "Are you serious?"

A: "Why shouldn't I be?"

D: "Well, it's just that... you know, not everybody felt that way. Jay didn't."

A: "He's an ape."

D: "He's just going through a stage. He's okay."

A: "If you say so."

Conversation fizzles. Home you go.

What a day. You start it off ready to strangle one ex-best friend, then you end up DEFENDING him to your other ex-best friend, who is slowly flickering away like a doused campfire that isn't quite out yet.

So maybe you should talk to Alex again. REALLY talk.

Maybe divorces DO have a delayed effect on some kids. Imagine how YOU would feel if YOUR parents were divorced.

Of course, if your parents divorced, you might not even know about it.

Do they have divorces in Ghana?

A Phone Conversation
In Which
Sunny's Law of Gender Conduct
Is Discussed

Sunny says, call Jay.

I say she's nuts. He should call ME!

Sunny says I'm a guy. He's a guy. Guys TALK TO EACH OTHER after they fight. They argue and explode and say things girls would never think of saying to each other, and then it all blows over and they play basketball.

I tell her I hate basketball.

She doesn't find that funny. She yells at me. She insists she's just using common sense.

I tell her I'll think about it.

Not good enough. She threatens to call me back in a half hour. If I haven't phoned Jay, or if I don't pick up, I am in the doghouse.

I BARK.

SHE HANGS UP.

OKAY, McCRAE, NOW WHAT?

DEPARTMENT OF TWISTS AND TURNS

I DID IT.

I REACHED JAY'S ANSWERING MACHINE.

THE REASON I GOT THE ANSWERING MACHINE WAS THAT JAY WAS OUT ON HIS BIKE.

THE PLACE HE WAS BIKING TO WAS MY HOUSE.

HE RANG THE DOORBELL.

I DIDN'T ANSWER.

HALF-PAST ANGER
QUARTER TO CRISIS

LOVE MAKES THE WORLD GO ROUND? WRONG.

GUILT DOES.

YOU DO SOMETHING LIKE NOT ANSWER THE DOOR AND SUDDENLY YOU FEEL LIKE A CRIMINAL, AND YOU WORRY THAT YOUR FRIEND ACTUALLY SAW YOU OR HEARD YOUR BREATHING WHILE HE WAS AT THE

DOOR, AND YOU PICTURE HIM STORMING AWAY ANGRILY AND KNOWING FINALLY BEYOND THE SHADOW OF A DOUBT THAT YOU ARE CHICKEN.

So you feel guilty. And you drive around town in your car, pretending to yourself that you're just going for a drive, but your eyes are constantly looking for him, and you figure if you see him you can casually say, "Hey, what's up?" And it'll seem like a coincidence.

But you don't see him. And that makes you feel worse.

So you finally drive to his house.

He's there. And he's all smiles.

"It's the Duckster! Duckopolis! Duckman! Duckorama!"

Slap. Slap. Slap. Slap. That's what each of those stupid names feels like.

He says right out: He was just over at your house, and you were out — which makes you gulp.

Then he says he has to show you something.

So he takes you around back, where there used to be an old, rusted basketball hoop on the garage. But now there's a new one, and the driveway has been widened and painted to look like a basketball court.

Jay is obviously very proud of this. And he makes you play basketball. He is bouncing or dribbling or whatever you call that, and you're hopping along beside him the way they teach you in gym class, even though you don't know why in the WORLD you're doing it, and you feel about as athletic as a turnip. And on top of that, you have to listen to Jay Adams's running

COMMENTARY ON HIMSELF: "HE FAKES . . . HE DRIVES TO THE BASELINE . . . HE SHOOTS . . . OFF THE RIM . . . THE OFFENSIVE REBOUND . . . HE PUMPS . . ."

THE BALL GOES OVER YOUR HEAD, SWISHES INTO THE BASKET, "YYYYESSSSS!" SHOUTS JAY, AND YOU HAVE HAD ENOUGH.

YOU TELL HIM YOU DON'T WANT TO PLAY.

BUT HE'S NOT REALLY LISTENING. HIS EYES ARE LOOKING OVER YOUR SHOULDER. AT THE DRIVEWAY.

WHAT A GREAT COINCIDENCE, JAY SAYS. HE HAS TO GO TO THE MALL, AND YOU'VE CONVENIENTLY BROUGHT YOUR CAR.

YOU SPUTTER. YOU START TO TELL HIM EXACTLY WHY YOU CAME OVER, BUT YOU CAN'T FIND THE WORDS, BECAUSE REALLY YOU DON'T KNOW, DO YOU? AND WHILE YOU'RE FUZZING OUT, HE'S ALREADY HALFWAY DOWN THE DRIVEWAY.

HOP IN. START. DRIVE. DUCKY MCCRAE, CHAUFFEUR TO THE WORLD.

AND YOU FINALLY TALK. ONLY IT DOESN'T QUITE GO THE WAY YOU EXPECTED. IT GOES SOMETHING LIKE THIS:

J: "YOU RECOVERED YET?" HE NUDGES YOU IN THE RIBS, WHICH IS THE WRONG THING TO DO TO A DRIVER, AND YOU SWERVE INTO THE LEFT LANE, NARROWLY MISSING AN ONCOMING CAR.

D: "@#$%&!!!" ON THE VERGE OF A HEART ATTACK.

J [LAUGHING HYSTERICALLY]: "DWI — DRIVING WHILE INTICKLE-ICATED!"

D: "OKAY. TO ANSWER YOUR QUESTION, NO. I HAVEN'T RECOVERED, IF YOU'RE TALKING ABOUT THE DINER —"

J: "LEEANN! WHAT A BABE!"

D: "Who?"

J: "LeeAnn? The girl at the diner? Hello? Earth to Duckomatic?"

D: "Oh! Well, you know, I had no idea —"

J: "SURPRISE! You should have seen the look on your face! HOW WAS THE RIDE HOME? — HAR HAR! Did you have a good time?"

D: "Okay...you want the truth?"

J: "No, just the DETAILS!"

D: "As a matter of fact, it was miserable. So was the dinner itself. I felt humiliated and awkward and trapped and I can't believe you did that to me."

Dead silence.

J [Deep sigh.]: "You blew it, huh?"

D: "Whaaat?"

J: "Duckmeister, if you want the girl, you have to MAKE CONVERSATION. You can't expect to score if you don't play the game —"

D: "I wasn't playing a game! I was having dinner!"

J: "You know what I mean. It's like a game. With rules and penalties and fake-outs and long shots — just like basketball. You have to talk the talk, walk the walk —"

D: "What you did was WRONG, Jay. You should have told me in advance. I thought it was going to be just you and me — not you, me, Lisa, and a total stranger."

J: "She's not a stranger. She's one of Lisa's best friends.

D: "I DON'T CARE!"

J: "Okay, so you didn't like her, it didn't work out, whatever. It happens. Now look, there's this other girl I know—"

D: "Jay, hello? Do you understand a word I'm saying?"

J: "I understand a lot. You didn't have a Valentine, dude. I'm concerned about you. Plenty of UGLY guys have Valentines. Why shouldn't YOU? You just have an inferiority complex or something, that's all. Nothing that a real girlfriend wouldn't cure. Anyway, her name is Barb—"

D: "Is this all you can think of—girls? What is with you? You NEVER used to be like this!"

J: "I'm trying to help you, Duckovich. Most guys would be thanking me. You think it was easy getting a babe like LeeAnn to go on a blind date? I had to talk you up. I said you were buff. Did you ever think YOU may be the one letting ME down?"

There's the mall. The gate to the garage is in sight, but you have NO INTENTION of going in, so you pull up to the curb and nearly shear off your whitewalls.

D: "YOU ARE MISSING THE WHOLE POINT, JAY!"

J: "YOU'RE the one missing the point! Of life!"

D: "Get out."

J: "Huh?"

D: "You heard me."

Jay unbuckles. Opens door. Steps out. Slams door.

You step on the gas. You are out of there.

THE END
C "D" McC
+
J "J" A
FRIENDSHIP
R.I.P.

EPILOGUE
A DAY LATER

WISHFUL THINKING.

IT WASN'T THE END. YOU DROVE AROUND TWO BLOCKS, FOLLOWING THE ONE-WAY STREETS. YOU PARKED. YOU WROTE DOWN YOUR THOUGHTS. THEN YOU WENT BACK.

JAY WAS STILL STANDING ON THE CURB.

AND YOU JUST DROVE UP AND TOLD HIM TO GET IN.

FOOL.

THAT WAS STUPID, McCRAE.

YOU COULD HAVE LEFT HIM THERE. HE WOULD HAVE GOTTEN HOME SOMEHOW — WALKED, OR MET SOME FRIEND IN THE MALL WHO DRIVES, SOMETHING.

YOU KNOW WHY YOU SHOULD HAVE DONE THAT? BECAUSE YOU

would've had time to cool off. And HE would've realized how serious you were.

But you didn't. There you were, trusty old Ducky, everybody's pal.

And Jay was laughing, as if he KNEW you would return. And he called you something like "Duckerino, Driver from Hell" as he climbed in, and that comment did NOT help your mood.

NOT

ONE

BIT.

And you wanted to smack yourself for your own stupidity, for being loyal to someone who just dumps and dumps and dumps on you.

Clamp. Step on the gas. Backs flat against the seat.

As you raced past the mall, Jay shouted out, "HEY, I HAVE SHOPPING TO DO."

You screeched to a stop and gave him a choice: shop by himself or catch a ride home.

He decided to stay in the car, and as you drove, he kept babbling on, sort of apologizing, sort of not, saying things that you had to tune out or you might drive off the road — hey, I didn't mean to upset you ... next time I'll let you know ... you should loosen up, Duckarino, have some fun ... Barbara is just your type, really, but I'm not going to force you ... what about Sunny, I can tell she likes you, but she's kind of out there, huh?

Not getting it AT ALL.

By the time you pulled up in front of Jay's house, you wanted to plant your foot in his side and kick him out the window.

As he opened the door, he had the NERVE to ask, "You still mad at me?"

And you discovered what you do when your brain starts flashing murderous thoughts.

You say nothing.

And the guy you just went out of your way to drive home shakes his head and mutters, "Some friend. You're just like Alex."

THAT's the thanks you get.

In Which Ducky McCrae
Finally Opens His Journal
After a Two-Day Vacation From Writing

It's Tuesday.

Note to yourself: don't ever get sick.

Just got back from the hospital. The smell of the place made you nauseated. Not to mention all the WHITE — white uniforms, white walls, white sheets. It all gave you a headache.

But when Sunny Winslow says, "Are you coming to the hospital with me after school or what?" you go with her.

Somehow, when SHE demands a ride, you don't feel like you're being taken for granted. Unlike some other friends who will remain nameless (his initials are Jay Adams). Plus, you know she's feeling nervous and upset about her mom, who has lung cancer.

As you walked through the hospital corridors, she took your arm and muttered, "I hate this."

You tried to smile and look reassuring. The two of you were arm in arm now, passing rooms full of people connected to IV tubes, and the strangest thoughts were going through your head. You imagined Jay spying on you, smiling and giving you a thumbs-up, like, "Hey, you finally got her." You imagined all the patients hobbling to their doors and applauding you. You shook all that out of your head — and then you were thinking about Mrs. Winslow and how you'd never met a person with cancer before. What would she look like? What would you say? WHAT IF SHE DIED WHILE YOU WERE IN THE ROOM? And you realized you were clutching Sunny's arm just as hard as she was clutching yours, and you knew you were scared of meeting Mrs. Winslow, but that was ridiculous because she's a human being and we all die sometime, and someday it'll be your turn and you wouldn't want anyone to dread seeing you — and you thought, "If this is how I'm feeling, imagine what must be going through Sunny's head right now."

Then you were in Mrs. Winslow's room. And she was there, watching TV. And she slowly turned to face you. And you saw her face for the first time.

She looks like a mom. A thin, older version of Sunny, with very little hair. She was very nice. We talked about school and TV shows. You were nervous when Sunny explained who you were — the guy who drove her home on the night she ran away — but Mrs. Winslow just smiled and said, "Thank you."

You stayed for awhile, chatting, nothing very memorable — and when you left, you felt relieved somehow.

Not Sunny. She was out of control.

She complained about her mom's linens. About the air-conditioning. The slow nursing staff. The food. The phone. The size of the room. The visiting hours. "You <u>see</u>?" she kept saying. "You <u>see</u>?"

You didn't know what you were supposed to see. But you knew Sunny needed a lot of yeses and that's-okays, so you gave them to her.

Finally, when you were outside, you put your arm around her and she started laughing. When you asked what was so funny, she just said, "I never cry," and then burst into tears.

You hugged her. You and she rocked back and forth in the parking lot, cars whizzing around you.

You realized something then. Something you should have known awhile ago.

Why worry about Alex and Jay? You have other friends who need you.

Sometimes You Wish
You Were in Eighth Grade

...Because if you were, then you would be able to actually have a decent conversation at lunch with Sunny and her friends, instead of walking past a table of Cro Mags who STILL call out, "Do you have a flower for ME, Ducky?" and throw you kisses, which makes you vow to drop your milk shake all over them someday even though it may cost you your life, and you're supposed to meet Jay, but he's not there, so you end up sitting with Alex, who is reading a horror novel and not eating. And he doesn't look up, so you ask him how it is, and he says, "Okay. I don't really know what it's about." And the only response you can think of — "Then why are you reading it?" — seems nasty so you shut up and eat.

And that's when you see Jay, halfway across the room with a hot-lunch tray.

You wave to him and shout, "Over here!" but he just glares at you.

And you finally have a conversation with Alex the Silent. Something along the lines of

D: "What's with him?"

A: "He won't sit here if I'm here."

D: "You guys have a fight or something?"

A: "Nahh, he's just a jerk. You can go sit with him. I want to be alone anyway."

D: "That's okay." [Start eating. Notice Alex's lunch bag is on the seat beside him.] "You had lunch already?"

A: "Nahh. Not hungry."

D: "You feeling all right?"

A: "No."

D: "Sick?"

A: "No."

D: "Bad mood?"

Alex tunes you out and continues reading. And you have that weird feeling again. Only this time the feeling tells you something is seriously wrong. But you're so frustrated and insulted and confused, all you can say is, "Hey, don't mind me, I don't exist."

A: "I didn't ask you to sit here."

D: "Right. You didn't. I'll just leave, okay?" [Stand up. Sit down.] "Okay, what is wrong, Alex?"

No answer.

D: "Talk to me, will you?"

A: "Why should I talk to you? You're not my therapist."

D: "You're seeing a therapist?"

A: "Maybe. None of your business."

D: [Chew, chew, chew, swallow.] "You know, there's nothing wrong with that. A lot of my friends have seen therapists."

A: "Yeah?"

D: "Ted used to see one — not anymore, but back when

Mom and Dad first started going on long trips. He was pretty young. Fifth grade, I think."

A: "I started way before that."

D: "When?"

A: "I don't know. When I was five or six. I don't remember NOT having a therapist."

Five or six.

This is news.

Big news.

You feel like you've been hit in the stomach.

Your mind is flashing back to your childhood. To the Old Alex. To the One Big Friendship of your life. To the person whose mind you could read. The guy you knew inside and out.

You were wrong.

He was keeping something from you. All those years, he was seeing a shrink. Going to appointments. Pouring out his problems to someone else.

And you didn't even notice.

WHEN? When did he go? Those times his mom would pick him up early on Saturday afternoons? She always said they were going shopping. You just assumed they shopped a lot.

And WHAT problems?

Except for those few months after the divorce, he always seemed pretty happy.

Or maybe he was just a good actor. Covering up his sadness. Fooling you. Completely.

You didn't know your best friend after all.

So you're thinking about this and not saying anything, and Alex is looking at you weirdly, and you're thinking maybe he can still read YOUR mind, and you're embarrassed as hell, and all you can think to say is, "Why?"

Which is not the right question, because Alex looks like he wants to cry, and he grabs his lunch, says, "Because I'm a psycho, I guess," and leaves.

You should run after him, but you're too stunned or something, which is too bad, because who should sit next to you but Jay.

He's grinning, and a shy-looking girl is with him.

Her name is Barbara, and he's told her all about you....

Midnight Musings

You WILL tell him off.

Again.

You were too chicken to do it over lunch. Not that you COULD anyway, with BARBARA standing right there, smiling at you, and your mind still on Alex and his secret life. All you could do was smile and say hi and try to act normal because she seemed like a nice enough person, as you watched Alex disappear down the hallway.

But you will tell Jay off, when you get the chance. If you have to yell at him a hundred times, you will.

DUCKY, YOU WILL NOT BE DUMPED ON.

But first things first.

The Alex department.

Some progress.

Talked to him after school. A little. He seemed in a hurry to get home. Maybe he had a shrink appointment.

Here's what I learned:

He's depressed. He's been depressed his whole life. It gets better, then it gets worse. That's why he's in therapy.

WHAT is he depressed about?

HE WON'T SAY.

The divorce?

You asked him that. He said no. He's handling that fine. Or so he says. Besides, he was in therapy BEFORE that.

Is it Paula? YOU wouldn't love having her for a younger sister. But PLENTY of people have bratty siblings. They don't have to go to a shrink for it for a whole lifetime.

School? Girl problems?

Is ANYTHING so serious that a person would need therapy for so long?

Therapy is supposed to HELP. You have a problem, you go, you talk, you get better. Like going to the doctor. Like what Ted did.

But this is different. This is almost a WHOLE LIFE.

A whole life with YOU in the middle of it. You, his best friend. His IGNORANT best friend, thinking you knew everything about him but not knowing a thing.

Why DIDN'T you know?

Why didn't he tell you? You could have listened to his problems and helped him. Maybe he'd be better off now.

His shrink sure hasn't helped.

Was the problem YOU?

Did you do something wrong?

Okay, you once squirted him in the eye with a water pistol and he said he wanted to kill you. That was in third grade.

You made Dad rent that horror movie when Alex and you were seven — and no one checked the rating, and it was so scary that Alex had nightmares for a week and his mom lectured you about unsuitable images. That was your fault.

You convinced him to sneak into Mrs. Kennedy's yard and she caught him but not you, and when she threatened to call the police and Alex was shaking with fear, you did nothing to help him.

My god, YOU WERE A LOUSY FRIEND. And what did you do during the Snyders' divorce? Nothing. You never wanted to talk about it. You didn't understand it, and you figured it wasn't your business.

How would YOU feel if you were a kid in the middle of your biggest life crisis, and your best friend just abandoned you?

You'd lose it.

You'd probably be just like Alex.

DUCKY. CHILL.

You are making a big deal out of this. At least he's talking to you. At least he's confiding something.

After a lifetime of keeping secrets from you.

Idea Over Breakfast

Here's a thought:

Alex is quiet and miserable.

Sunny is loud and miserable.

They might actually get along.

Maybe they should meet.

Upon Further Reflection
Over Lunch

What are you, nuts?

In Which
Christopher Discovers
That He Is Still Enrolled in School

You should have given Ms. Patterson TWO carnations on Valentine's Day, Ducky.

Maybe you wouldn't have flunked the math test.

But you didn't. And you did.

You are in deep doo-doo.

A Passage of Several Days

...And you are still alive.

You even know the difference between a cosine and a sine. Possibly. Your brain is fried from math study, which is why you haven't written.

Ms. Patterson knows you write in this journal during class. If you open it again in math, she confiscates it.

Which is why you are spending lunch period hunched in the corner of the cafeteria, scribbling away.

LOTS TO TELL. WHERE TO BEGIN?

Okay.

Part One. Jay.

Just when you think it's safe to make him your enemy, Jay surprises you.

He comes to your house with a brand-new chess set and asks if you want to play. CHESS! By the time you pick yourself up off the floor, laughing, he looks like a hurt puppy. "I thought you LIKED chess," he says. So you reassure him that you DO like it, and you invite him in to play, and he's the worst player in the world but he LOVES it, and you teach him a defense or two and he calls you a genius, and all of a sudden you think he's an okay guy after all.

And after you've beaten him a second time, he agrees to buy you dinner for no reason at all. And when you get to China Wok, you ask him why he's doing all this stuff — the unexpected visit, the chess, the food — and he says he's just trying to be friends again. And he tells you he's worried about you, because you look mad all the time. "Aren't we still buddies, Duckeroni?"

And you have to admit, this makes you feel pretty great, even though you have to tell him you HATE his nicknames.

You explain you've been a maniac lately because of the math. You haven't really BEEN mad, you've just LOOKED mad. Which is kind of the truth, but kind of not, because Jay Adams has not exactly been on your list of top ten favorite people these days. Not even top thousand.

Anyway, he seems relieved, and he offers to help you with homework but you say no, because HIS help is likely to REALLY sink your grades. And now that you're talking like human beings, you finally unload how you feel about his matchmaking — calmly, rationally — and he's sort of getting it, sort of not, asking you stuff like, "Well, what kind of girl do you like?" when Sunny walks in with Dawn.

End of conversation. Jay acts like he has never seen a more beautiful sight in the world than Dawn Schafer. Dawn and Sunny sit down with us, and Jay asks Dawn a million questions. She's acting really friendly, probably just humoring him, but they're having a great time.

And you're thinking, hmmm, Dawn and Jay? You wouldn't have predicted it, but maybe opposites do attract. And in a funny way, you are jealous, McCrae. Because life seems so easy for Jay. Even though he can be a pigheaded goon, people like him. Girls like him. And why not? He's outgoing. He's friendly. He's funny. When you get past all the stuff that makes you crazy, you find a sweet guy. But that's not the worst part. The WORST part, the thing you really envy, is that it takes SO LITTLE to make him happy.

The Secret to Contentment, According to Jay Adams: Meet a girl.

The Secret to Contentment, According to Ducky McCrae: Worry about how you look in the morning, because even though you can't bring yourself to wear boring conservative

CLOTHES, YOU DON'T WANT TO RISK SETTING OFF THE CRO MAGS. AND MAKE SURE YOU DON'T BOUNCE TOO MUCH AS YOU'RE WALKING INTO SCHOOL, BECAUSE MARCO THE CRO MAG KING WILL SAY YOU'RE FLITTING, WHICH MAKES EVERYONE LAUGH. IF YOU SURVIVE THAT, YOU'RE OFF TO A GOOD START, AND IF YOU'RE LUCKY YOU'LL HAVE A FEW LAUGHS WITH YOUR 13-YEAR-OLD FRIENDS, THE ONLY ONES WHO SEEM TO APPRECIATE YOU, AND WHEN YOU GO HOME, YOU'LL FIND THAT YOUR BROTHER HAS NOT LEFT THE MILK OUT OF THE FRIDGE ALL DAY AND HAS ACTUALLY BOUGHT A FEW GROCERIES AND MAYBE RUN A LOAD OF LAUNDRY WITH SOME OF YOUR STUFF IN IT. THAT'S CONTENTMENT. AND THAT'S PATHETIC.

SO YOU'RE THINKING THIS, AND YOU'RE GETTING MAD AND FRUSTRATED AT YOURSELF FOR BEING JEALOUS, AND YOUR FRIEND DAWN, WHO OTHERWISE HAS ALWAYS BEEN PRETTY SENSIBLE, SEEMS KIND OF FASCINATED BY JAY, KIND OF ATTRACTED TO HIM, AND THEN...

WE ALL ORDER FOOD, AND HE ASKS FOR SPARE RIBS AND SWEET AND SOUR BEEF.

OF COURSE, HE HAS NO IDEA THAT DAWN IS THE WORLD'S NUMBER ONE HEALTH FOOD NUT, WHO EATS ABSOLUTELY NO RED MEAT.

HER FACE CLOUDS OVER. HER EYES NARROW. SHE MUTTERS, "EW."

DOES JAY LEAVE IT ALONE? NO. HE ASKS QUESTIONS, FINDS OUT ABOUT HER EATING HABITS, AND LOOKS AT HER LIKE SHE'S FROM NEPTUNE. THEN HE SAYS THINGS LIKE "HOW CAN YOU NOT LIKE A JUICY RED STEAK?" AND "AREN'T YOU HUNGRY ALL THE TIME?" AND DAWN DOESN'T WANT TO MAKE A SCENE, SO SHE'S TRYING TO CHANGE THE SUBJECT, BUT YOU CAN SEE HER GETTING ANGRIER AND ANGRIER.

You no longer feel so jealous. But is that right? Should you be GLOATING because Jay is under attack?

Why not?

Finally Sunny manages to get us all talking about movies — only Jay is chewing the spare ribs lovingly and saying, "Mmmmm" while looking straight at Dawn, who is not amused, and you realize your 8th-grade friends are much more mature than some of your OLDER friends, and before you know it, everyone is serious — including Jay — because Sunny is talking about her mom's cancer.

This sure doesn't brighten things, but Jay has stopped his doofus act and is listening intently. He comments that Alex's aunt had lung cancer, and you remember that. You remember how Jay and you comforted Alex when she died, and how Jay cried, and you feel this pang in your chest for the old days, when we were all so close.

It's a pretty intense dinner. Afterward, you drive Jay home, and one of the first things he says is, "She's perfect!"

You explain that if he even THOUGHT about asking Dawn out, he would probably have to abstain from meat-eating for a few months first, before she'd even look at him again.

But no. He's talking about SUNNY.

He is saying that she's perfect for Alex.

And this, finally, leads to

PART TWO. ALEX.

But it is almost time for next period and you haven't eaten anything yet, so you sign off temporarily.

No Longer Hungry
Just Bored with English Class

...So you pretend to be writing the Great American Essay, when in reality you are going back to where you left off.

Yesterday. Okay, you're home from the China Wok. You're thinking about Jay's comment.

Matching up Sunny and Alex. It's so JAY. So mind-bogglingly WRONG. But just the fact that he showed concern for Alex is a good thing. And THAT's what you're thinking about. Maybe the three of you are NOT on three different planets. Maybe you can all be best friends again.

And really, there's something about the idea that isn't so stupid. It might be good for Alex and Sunny to know each other. Not in a dating sense, just in a hanging-out-as-friends sense. Sunny's the ONLY person who would understand the kind of depression Alex must be having.

And Alex might be just the one to reach Sunny when she gets into one of her dark, angry moods.

So you figure you'll invite them both to hang out with you at the beach Saturday. You call them. Sunny doesn't sound thrilled that Alex is invited. Alex says he's sick of the beach and he doesn't like meeting strangers.

It's not easy, but you twist their arms.

You tell them both, "It's important to me that you come."

Which is true.

And they agree.

Another good deed by Ducky.

Saturday at Venice Beach

You picked up Alex first. He looked about as happy as he would be if he were going to an all-day math fair.

He complained about how early it was.

He complained that it was too cold for the beach.

He complained that he was tired.

You were surprised he even got into the car.

But he did, and you drove off, singing along with the radio, and when the station played an oldie that you and Alex used to love, you shouted out, "Remember this?"

But he was slumped in the backseat, eyes closed. As you pulled up to the Winslows', Sunny BOUNCED out the front door. In such a good mood.

Then she saw the corpse in the backseat.

"Oh, uh, hi, is he . . . ?"

You nudged Alex awake. You introduced him to Sunny.

He just grunted.

Sunny climbed into the front seat, and you covered for Alex. You said he was probably up late studying, or something stupid like that.

Sunny is SO cool. She just took over the talking:

S: "I am JEALOUS. I could use some sleep too."

A: "Mmmph."

S: "I was up all night. My mom's home from the hospital. She has lung cancer."

A [finally sits up.]: "Oh. Wow. Too bad."

S: "Thanks. It's hard. She's really bony now, and she has these bedsores from the hospital bed, which is made out of, like, marble or something. So she gets these pains, and then she wakes up, and I haven't been sleeping well lately, so if I hear her, I am UP!"

A: "I know what you mean. ANYTHING can wake me up."

For that moment, you thought you were a genius.

They were talking. CONNECTING. Sunny was going on and on about cancer and chemotherapy and radiation treatments. You could see Alex's face in the rearview mirror. He was actually interested. Concerned.

A: "My aunt Wendy? She had lung cancer too. And she'd given up smoking when she was young."

S: "My mom too!"

A: "And Wendy had chemo and stuff. She lost her hair."

S: "How's she doing now?"

A: "She died."

No.

NO.

The air in the car froze.

S: "Oh. Well, you know, they've had a lot of success with combining the chemo and the radiation."

A: "That's what they told us too."

S: "But nowadays they do it better. It's not like it used to be."

A: "My aunt died only a year ago. I mean, not that your mom's going to <u>die</u>, I just meant it didn't happen, like, way in the past."

S: "Uh-huh."

Finally, FINALLY, you had the brains to turn on the radio.

You listened to the top 40. And no one said another word until you got to the beach.

You kept trying. You treated everyone to lunch. You joked around.

But the chemistry was dead.

After we ate, we put on our blades. Sunny went in one direction, Alex the other.

You bladed around in circles.

The story of your life.

Department of
Second Chances

It's Saturday night and your brother is having a huge party, which means drunken guys taking over the house, and girls with big hair and makeup, and lousy music and snide comments, and usually at least two broken appliances, so YOU ARE OUT OF HERE.

But first, a word or two in your trusty journal.

You didn't expect to be in one piece right now, considering what happened this afternoon, namely that you tried to bring two friends together and found out that they truly did have one thing in common — the ability to depress each other.

So when Sunny called afterward, you must have said, "I'm sorry" a hundred times. You fell all over yourself explaining why you did it.

Sunny listened. She did not hang up on you or scream bloody murder. Instead, she said, "I don't know WHAT you're talking about. I was calling to say thanks."

A joke, you assumed.

But no. She was moved. By the GESTURE. She said that friends don't always think of perfect solutions, but they try, and that's what counts. She said her mom has a support group — and what were YOU doing but trying to find her a supportive friend?

For a 13-year-old, Sunny is pretty amazing.

So you felt good about yourself after that, and you bravely called Alex. He wasn't home. His mom said he'd gone off on his bike to Las Palmas.

Time to go. Ted's outside. He has about a hundred of his friends in the car with him. In a moment, he will start blowing his horn, because he'll want my car out of the driveway, so HE can pull up and avoid the extra ten feet he'd have to walk to the kitchen door.

There it goes.

Bye.

In the Kitchen
Sunday Night,
Dazed and Confused,
With Two Pens
Because This Could Last a Lonnnnng Time

You are sitting in a war zone.

You just had to peel your journal from an unidentified sticky stain on the kitchen table. But considering that the REST of the table is blanketed with uneaten food that would take hours to clean, you have covered the stain with a plastic bag, in which there were once English muffins.

Two of the muffins lay swollen in a bowl full of water in the sink.

Ted is a slob. His friends are pigs. And none of them are around to yell at.

So, McCrae, you will do what you always do — try to ignore the mess and deal with it tomorrow.

You have enough to deal with today.

You COULD have avoided it. When you left the house earlier, you COULD have just taken a long drive. Hung out at the mall. Gone to Sunny's house.

But no.

Instead you decide to drive to Las Palmas.

Why? Because Alex is there, and you think he'll be happy and thankful, like Sunny. And it feels so nice to be THANKED. You could get addicted to it.

So you find him, in that same spot by the bridge, and you cheerfully say hi and sit beside him.

He doesn't say a thing. Just sits, looking at the creek, pulling grass.

You talk — Nice day. Cool breeze. Check out the turtle. And you ask questions — Did you have an okay time at the beach? Sunny's a good person, isn't she? Are you going to speak to me?

And his expression never changes once, just a total blank, until right in the middle of something — some dumb, harmless question of yours — he pushes you.

With both hands, and hard.

"Can't you ever shut up?" he shouts.

You stammer something, but you're too shocked to make any sense.

Alex is furious. He tells you to get out of here. He calls you nasty names.

And then he's sitting next to you, crying.

You ask if he's okay, if he wants to talk. He's so upset, he can't even answer.

So you pat him reassuringly on the back. He doesn't react at all, and you both just sit there.

Finally he says that he felt you were ignoring him at the beach. Like you brought Sunny along because you didn't want to hang out with him alone. Which made him feel kind of like a charity case. And now you know. You DID hurt his feelings. You were a fool to think he'd THANK you.

But in a way, you're relieved, because you weren't sure Alex HAD feelings anymore.

So you apologize, and Alex wipes his eyes, and you remember the time years ago when his gerbil died and you both buried it in the park not far from here.

And then Alex actually reminds you about that. HE was thinking about it too!

A moment.

A real Ducky and Alex moment.

The first one in what seems like years.

You want to put your arm around his shoulder, but you

DON'T. YOU MIGHT HAVE IF IT WERE A FEW YEARS AGO, WHEN YOU WERE YOUNGER AND KIDS DIDN'T LAUGH AT YOU FOR STUFF LIKE THAT. BUT IN THE DISTANCE YOU HEAR SOME LOUD SHOUTING, AND THE LAST THING YOU NEED IS FOR A PACK OF CRO MAGS TO FIND THE TWO OF YOU ON A PARK BENCH, HUGGING.

So YOU ASK HIM WHAT'S ON HIS MIND.

AND IT'S AS IF THE TEARS HAVE WASHED AWAY A LAYER OF TOUGH SKIN, BECAUSE ALEX STARTS TALKING IN A FAMILIAR VOICE THAT YOU RECALL FROM THE DISTANT PAST, SOFT AND SLOW, THE WAY HE USED TO TALK WHEN HE WAS VERY SERIOUS.

HE TELLS YOU HE HAS TROUBLE GETTING OUT OF BED IN THE MORNINGS. SOMETIMES HIS MOM ACTUALLY HAS TO SLAP HIM, OR DRAG HIM UP. HE'S ALWAYS TIRED THROUGHOUT THE DAY. WHEN HE GETS TO SCHOOL, HE CAN'T KEEP HIS EYES OPEN IN CLASS.

HE TELLS YOU HE HAS NOT DONE ONE HOMEWORK ASSIGNMENT THIS YEAR, AND THAT HIS GUIDANCE COUNSELOR IS ALMOST CERTAIN HE'LL BE LEFT BACK, BUT HE DOESN'T CARE BECAUSE TENTH GRADE, ELEVENTH, NINTH, FOURTH — THEY'RE ALL THE SAME TO HIM.

HE SAYS THAT HE'S BEEN ON DIFFERENT MEDICATIONS FOR DEPRESSION, AND SOME OF THEM WORK OKAY FOR AWHILE, BUT HE FORGETS TO TAKE THEM OR THEY WEAR OFF OR THE DOCTOR DOESN'T REFILL THE PRESCRIPTION.

HE CLAIMS HE'S NOT UPSET ABOUT HIS PARENTS' DIVORCE ANYMORE. HE DOESN'T CARE IF EITHER OF THEM GETS REMARRIED.

HE TELLS YOU HE'S MAKING HIS SISTER'S LIFE MISERABLE. SHE DOESN'T EVEN LIKE TO BRING FRIENDS HOME BECAUSE HE WEIRDS THEM

OUT, JUST BY BEING THERE. He's also making his mom's life miserable. She doesn't know what to do with him. Half the time she's pleading, half the time she's yelling.

THAT, he says, is about the only thing he cares about. That he's annoying other people. He hates doing it, but he can't help himself. Sometimes he feels like there's another person inside him, someone he doesn't know, someone who's taking him over, making him do and say things he'd never think of normally.

And you're just sitting there, stunned, not knowing what to say. You're thinking this is good in a way, good that Alex is being emotional, good that he's letting it all out.

You try to tell him that, but you're not sure he hears you. He's in his own world, looking at the ground, and now he starts speaking even softer, in a tiny voice. He's saying that he did not sleep at all last night. He was tired, he went to bed, his eyes closed, he felt himself drifting off, and then, BANG, he was wide awake. He thought about his parents and how HE was the cause of the breakup, he thought about how he was sure his sister hated him, he thought about all the homework he hadn't done. He thought and thought and thought and all the images from those thoughts were like a huge movie screen that slowly began curving around him and trapping him in the middle, and he would then get up and walk around the house but the darkness made him feel worse, so he'd turn on the TV but all he'd find were creepy old movies and stupid cheerful infomercials that reminded him how bad his life was, so he'd go

BACK TO BED AND THE THOUGHTS WOULD START UP AGAIN — AND SOON HE FELT AS IF HE WERE RACING THE SUNRISE, AND THEN THERE IT WAS, PEEKING IN THROUGH THE BLINDS AND THAT WAS IT, HE WAS UP FOR GOOD, AND HE DIDN'T REALLY WANT TO GO TO THE BEACH BUT IT WAS BETTER THAN STAYING IN HIS HOUSE.

So HE GOT DRESSED AND ATE BREAKFAST AND WAITED FOR YOU, THINKING HE COULD TALK TO YOU ABOUT THE DREAM, BUT SOMEHOW HE'D FORGOTTEN THAT SUNNY WAS COMING ALONG, AND WHEN HE REALIZED IT, HE WANTED TO GO BACK HOME BUT AT THAT POINT HE DIDN'T CARE ENOUGH TO ARGUE, BECAUSE HE WAS TOO WEARY, AS IF HIS ENTIRE BODY HAD BEEN SCRAPED AND PEELED.

WHAT CAN YOU SAY TO THAT EXCEPT "WOW" AND "TOO BAD" AND "I'M SORRY," AND YOU TRY TO THINK OF OTHER THINGS, BUT THEY ALL SOUND RIDICULOUS, THEN YOU STOP TRYING BECAUSE ALEX IS IGNORING YOU, AND HIS VOICE IS ALL CHOKED UP AND HE'S SAYING HE CAN'T SPEND ANOTHER NIGHT LIKE THAT, HE CAN'T CAN'T CAN'T AND IF IT EVER STARTS TO HAPPEN AGAIN HE WILL JUST DIE.

AND YOU KNOW PEOPLE TAKE PILLS TO HELP THEM SLEEP, BUT YOU DON'T WANT TO SUGGEST THAT, BECAUSE HIS SHRINK'S JOB IS TO FIGURE THAT STUFF OUT.

So YOU ASK IF HE'S STILL IN THERAPY. AND HE SAYS YEAH, SORT OF, BUT HE'S BEEN SKIPPING A LOT OF SESSIONS LATELY. AND THAT MAKES HIS MOM ANGRY, BECAUSE SHE CAN BARELY AFFORD DR. WELSCH TO BEGIN WITH, BUT ALEX CAN'T HELP SKIPPING BECAUSE HE'S BORED TO DEATH WITH THE SESSIONS AND THEY'RE NOT HELPING ANYWAY.

Which sure doesn't sound promising to you, but you don't dare say that to Alex in his state.

Instead you just sit. Silently.

You toss a stone into the creek. Fish scatter, a duck noisily flaps its wings, and a sunning turtle draws in its head. As the ripples glide outward, the animals settle down until you can't even tell a crisis ever occurred.

Alex is watching this too. Neither of you wants to move. Neither of you wants to talk.

And you stay like that for the rest of the afternoon.

In Which
School, Once Again,
Raises Its Ugly Head

As if I didn't have enough to worry about — now I'm flunking English. Is this ironic, or what — I've finally raised my math grades, but I'm failing the only subject I LIKE.

Did I KNOW I was supposed to read <u>Julius Caesar</u>? Did I KNOW an essay was due today?

Where was I when Ms. Turnbull gave out the assignment?

Probably in class, but writing in THIS!

I am in a FOUL mood.

Sunny noticed this. She asked me if something was wrong.

She's the only person who cares, I guess. I thanked her but I didn't want to complain. She has enough on her mind. So I just told her I was flunking English, that's all.

She thought that was funny. She said I'm starting to sound like HER. She guaranteed me that I'll be cutting classes soon.

Great. And I'M supposed to be a good role model for HER.

I don't know what is happening to me.

The Cro Mags think I'm a sissy bookworm. My teachers think I'm a slacker. My 8th-grade friends look up to me and I let them down. My 10th-grade friends feel betrayed.

I'M TRYING TO DO THE BEST I CAN, and my life gets worse every day.

I CAN'T TAKE THIS.

I need advice. I need to talk to someone.

But who?

Not Jay. He'll just tell me I need a girlfriend.

Not Ted. He doesn't have time for me. He's too busy figuring out creative ways to destroy the house.

Mom and Dad are on the other side of the world. And Alex is halfway to Mars.

Maybe Dr. Welsch has an opening. Ha ha.

Anyway, enough of this. I have to study Julius.

"To be or not to be..."

Or is that another play?

Whatever.

Up in the Vista Hills
Overlooking the Valley
With a Full Stomach
And Feeling, for the First Time in Awhile,
Like a Human Being

It is so dark and quiet up here. A little cool, but that's all right. Below me, Palo City stretches out, and I can see lights flicking off as people go to bed.

The old telescope isn't here anymore. It's just four bolts in some cracked pavement now, next to the concrete block where I used to stand when I was a kid, and I'd look through and never be able to see much because of the smog and the fact that Dad never taught me how to FOCUS the thing.

Oh well.

It's so nice to relax and think of all this stuff.

Enjoy it while it lasts, Ducky.

You sure didn't expect it. Not the way this day started. It could have been a total washout.

The pop quiz in math was bad enough. But the chem lab experiment was worse, only because the chemicals STANK, which gave you a splitting headache. Then came the read-aloud of J Caesar in English class, and OF COURSE you were the bad guy, Brutus, and all the Cro Mags were snickering about THAT, after they got over their hilarious pantomime of friends,

Romans, and countrymen "lending their ears" by ripping them off and howling in pain.

THEY ARE FIFTEEN YEARS OLD. HAVEN'T THEY GROWN OUT OF STUFF LIKE THIS? (And you think you're immature?)

Not only that, but Alex was absent today, and you can't help but be worried.

So with all THAT on your mind, you were not too excited when Sunny asked you to go to the hospital AGAIN after school — but you had to say yes, because she said she needed help bringing her mom home after some tests.

Then, when you arrived at the hospital, you found out that two members of Mrs. Winslow's support group were there, and so was Mr. Winslow. So Sunny's mom DIDN'T need the help, and you were just there because Sunny was nervous and SHE needed support.

At first you didn't mind because you wanted to help. The support group people were really nice, and they assumed you were Sunny's boyfriend and treated you like part of the family, and Mrs. Winslow was very thankful, and you did hold her arm as she went from the bed to the wheelchair, so you didn't feel TOTALLY useless.

Afterward you were ready to go home and try to catch up on schoolwork, but Sunny asked you to drive her back to her house. She could have gone in her dad's car, but no, she insisted. And you figured, hey, what are friends for? — and all the way back, Sunny DID NOT STOP COMPLAINING. Her mom's sickness

WAS DRAINING HER, HER DAD WAS BEING CRABBY, HER LIFE WAS HORRIBLE and DEPRESSING AND ALL SHE WANTED TO DO WAS RUN AWAY.

So you joked with her and reassured her and told her she was great, but your heart wasn't in it, because all you could think about were Alex's problems and the Cro Mags and Jay and math class and Julius Caesar and Ghana and YOUR OWN DEPRESSING LIFE, but you told yourself not to be selfish, and you listened to Sunny go on and on, being sarcastic and complaining about her poor, sick mom, and even though you didn't mean to be rude, you said, "At least YOUR mom is around."

Major, major mistake.

Right away you wished you could take that back. You wished you could catch the words in midair, the way a frog uses its tongue to catch a fly.

And Sunny was staring at you, her mouth open, and you knew you had just blown it. Your best friendship in the world, flushed down the toilet.

Before you could say anything, Sunny was on your case. She reminded you that YOUR mom is healthy and she's only away TEMPORARILY and how could you possibly compare the two — and you fell all over yourself apologizing, making excuses, telling her you didn't mean what you said, you just wanted her to be happy and enjoy life and stop feeling sorry for herself — STOP FEELING SORRY FOR YOURSELF, could you possibly have picked a worse

THING TO SAY, McCRAE? — AND SUNNY WENT OFF ON A TANGENT AND YOU WEREN'T REALLY LISTENING, BECAUSE ALL YOU COULD THINK WAS WHAT A BAD FRIEND YOU WERE AND YOU NEVER SHOULD HAVE AGREED TO DRIVE SUNNY HOME BECAUSE YOU DON'T KNOW HOW TO KEEP YOUR BIG MOUTH SHUT.

AND FINALLY SUNNY'S VOICE STOPPED SOUNDING LIKE WORDS AND BECAME MORE LIKE A NOISE, LIKE FINGERNAILS SCRAPING A BLACKBOARD, AND YOU NEEDED TO KEEP CONCENTRATING ON THE ROAD BUT THAT WAS HARD BECAUSE YOU FELT ALL THIS PRESSURE, THINKING ABOUT HOW YOU SHOULD HAVE BEEN HOME STUDYING BUT INSTEAD YOU WERE SOLVING SOMEONE ELSE'S PROBLEMS, PUTTING SOMEONE ELSE'S LIFE FIRST, AS USUAL, AND DON'T YOUR FRIENDS SEE THAT YOU'RE A PERSON TOO? AND THEN YOU THOUGHT, HOW CAN THEY WHEN YOU JUMP AT THEIR REQUESTS AND ACT LIKE YOU'RE THE HAPPIEST PERSON IN THE WORLD AND OF COURSE THEY'RE GOING TO TAKE ADVANTAGE UNLESS YOU PUT YOUR FOOT DOWN.

"BE QUIET!" YOU YELLED.

IT WAS ALMOST AS IF SOMEONE ELSE HAD CLIMBED INSIDE YOU AND STARTED SHOUTING. AND ONCE YOU STARTED, YOU COULDN'T STOP. YOU BLURTED OUT HOW YOU WERE FEELING — HOW SCARED AND TENSE AND WORRIED YOU WERE, AND BEFORE YOU KNEW IT, YOU WERE TELLING HER ABOUT THE CRO MAGS AND ALEX AND JAY. AND SUNNY WAS QUIETLY LISTENING AND SAYING "REALLY?" AND "OH, DUCKY," AND "WHY DIDN'T YOU TELL ME?" AND BY THE TIME YOU TURNED ONTO HER STREET YOUR EYES WERE SO MISTED UP YOU COULD BARELY SEE THE ROAD.

AND BOOM, YOU FELT ANGRY AT YOURSELF, AND GUILTY, BECAUSE

here was Sunny, all upset about her mom, and you couldn't just let her vent, could you? Okay, she's feeling all this self-pity, but you do the same thing and SHE HAS AN EVEN BETTER REASON TO DO IT THAN YOU so you shouldn't judge her, you should let her complain, THIS IS NOT ABOUT YOU, ANYWAY.

And those last words remind you of Mom and Dad, the way they'd say that to you sometimes when you were upset, and you never understood it, because you thought EVERYTHING was about you — and you think of them, and of home, and it's the last place you want to go right now, so when Sunny asks you to come inside her house, you say yes.

Sunny's mom is lying on a sofa in the Winslows' living room. Mr. Winslow is on the phone, and the support group friends are making dinner in the kitchen. So you and Sunny sit with her mom, and you begin telling stories about school and doing imitations of various students and teachers, and Mrs. Winslow is cracking up and saying how talented you are and comparing you to Robin Williams (!), which eggs you on — and soon everyone else is in the living room, and they're all your audience, laughing at all your jokes, and you feel great. You feel APPRECIATED. So when Mr. Winslow asks you to stay for dinner, you say yes because you know the alternative at the McCrae house is Cheerios, in milk that's probably been left out since Ted came home from school.

The support groupers are great cooks.

The meal is the best you've had in months.

And the drive up into Vista Hills — sitting here, writing, with the breeze blowing through the open windows — that's the perfect dessert.

In Which You Ask the Question: So Why Couldn't the Day Have Ended There?

You are a maniac.

Your hands are filthy. Your shirt is clammy with sweat. You smell.

It is 11:21, and you have spent the entire night CLEANING. Why did you bother coming home?

WHAT A DISGUSTING MESS this place is! Cigarette butts in the toilet tank. Fungus growing under the fridge. Chewing gum on the kitchen floor. A rock in the stove that looks like it was once a hamburger.

Clothes you forgot you even owned. Clothes that were once Ted's but have been lying around so long they probably fit you. Clothes that don't belong to anyone you know and you don't know what they're doing here. You don't WANT to know.

HOW DID IT GET THIS BAD? You were HERE the whole time. Didn't you notice?

You did notice. You just didn't care. Because it was just the way things were. Life with Ted and Ducky.

It hit you tonight, though. You opened the door, and — WHAM — the stench hit you.

Your house SMELLS.

It's like a combination locker room, laundry hamper, and Dumpster from the back of a restaurant.

And up until then, you'd felt so good. Driving into the hills was relaxing. And the meal at Sunny's — you'd forgotten how much fun it could be to just sit around eating and talking.

It's such normal stuff. But it's stuff you haven't done in months. Since Mom and Dad left. Which is so weird because you never think life is so great when they're here — and maybe it isn't, but it sure feels better than it does now.

For one thing, when they're here, it feels like you live in a HOME.

You look forward to coming back to a HOME. A HOME doesn't stink.

SUNNY has a home.

You have a HOLE.

She has a FAMILY.

You have a

What? What do you have?

What are Ted and you?

It's like, when Mom and Dad leave, you say: Okay, family's

OVER FOR AWHILE. SUSPENDED ANIMATION. DON'T DO ANYTHING UNTIL THEY COME BACK.

YOU AND TED DON'T TALK TO EACH OTHER MUCH. YOU DON'T DO ANYTHING MUCH. YOU JUST COME HOME, SLEEP, GO TO SCHOOL. LIKE YOU'RE WAITING FOR SOMEONE TO TELL YOU WHAT ELSE TO DO. SOMEONE TO TELL YOU HOW TO ACT. LIKE YOU'RE BOTH PARALYZED.

SO HOW ARE YOU SUPPOSED TO ACT? IT'S NOT LIKE YOU CAN BUY A BOOK ABOUT THIS. THERE'S NO HOMEMAKING GUIDE FOR VIRTUAL ORPHANS.

SO YOU CLEANED.

THE HOUSE STILL LOOKS DISGUSTING. BUT IT'S A START.

MAYBE YOU'LL TALK TO TED ABOUT THIS TOMORROW.

MAYBE NOT. YOU DON'T NEED ANOTHER ARGUMENT.

WHAT
HAVE
YOU
DONE?

YOU COULDN'T HAVE KEPT YOUR MOUTH SHUT?

YOU HAD TO TELL JAY, OF ALL PEOPLE, ABOUT YOUR HOUSECLEANING? YOU HAD TO PAINT THIS PICTURE OF YOURSELF FLITTING FROM ROOM TO ROOM, PICKING UP OLD UNDERWEAR, PUTTING ON AN apron like Suzy Homemaker to do a stack of dishes that was almost glued together with dried food?

You didn't ASSUME he was going to tell everybody in school? That this would NOT help your reputation at all?

Duh.

NOW what?

Now Jay is coming over after school to HELP you. And he's bringing Lisa, a broom, and a can of Lysol.

And...Bud.

Bud the Cro Mag.

Why?

You don't know why. Jay secretly hates you, you guess.

Jay insisted that Bud is OK. Which you accepted. You said FINE — but WHY ON EARTH MAKE HIM COME TO YOUR HOUSE TO CLEAN UP, OF ALL RIDICULOUS THINGS? — and Jay insisted that he was talking to Bud the other day, and JUST CASUALLY in conversation your name came up, and Bud said he FELT BAD about the way their pals treat you, and so Jay said, okay, if you want to do something about it, let's help my buddy Duckster clean his trashed house, and Bud was psyched about it.

DOES THIS MAKE SENSE?

No, it doesn't.

WHY was he psyched? Does he want to do research? Take photos? Infiltrate the house of Ducky and report to the Cro Mags, so they can humiliate you EVEN MORE?

And what's worse, YOU COULDN'T SAY NO. You tried, but Jay just railroaded you. He insisted that he was trying to help. And you know what happens when Jay "helps."

McCrae, your days are numbered.

The Great McCrae
Cleanup

You're home alone, after school. You're in a blind panic.

You consider calling a cleaning service. You consider calling Jay and saying you're sick. Locking the door and running away. Setting fire to the whole thing.

But instead you stand there in the house, frozen.

You figure: Cleaning the place up before they get here might make Bud angry, because then he'd be coming over for no reason. But leaving it filthy might make him hate you, because he'd have so much work to do.

You try to imagine you're a Cro Mag, living alone with your brother. How would YOUR house look?

Like a prehistoric cave. Finger paintings of bison on the walls.

So you decide to do nothing because maybe a messy house is a good thing, like a badge of honor, and just the thought of this makes you realize you are OVERTHINKING and MAKING THIS TOO

IMPORTANT, AND MAYBE JAY WAS RIGHT AND BUD HAS NOTHING BETTER TO DO THAN COME OVER AND HELP OUT A FRIEND OF A FRIEND.

STILL, YOU'RE CONSTANTLY LOOKING OUT THE WINDOW FOR TED. MAYBE — JUST MAYBE — YOUR BROTHER WOULD COME HOME THE ONE DAY YOU NEED HIM. BUT NO. HE'S PROBABLY STUFFING HIS FACE WITH PIZZA AND HAVING A GREAT TIME IN YOUR MOMENT OF HUMILIATION.

THE DOORBELL RINGS, AND YOUR HAND SHAKES AS YOU REACH FOR THE KNOB. YOU OPEN THE DOOR, TRYING TO LOOK AS MACHO AS POSSIBLE.

"YO," YOU SAY. "'TSUP?"

BUT JAY'S NOT LOOKING AT YOU. HE'S STARING AT THE ROOM BEHIND YOU AND HIS FIRST COMMENT IS "WHAT HAPPENED?"

LISA'S FACE IS ALL TWISTED IN SHOCK AND DISGUST, AS IF SHE JUST WALKED INTO A FERTILIZER SALE AT SEARS.

BEHIND HER IS BUD McNALLY — AND HE LOOKS AMUSED. HE'S LAUGHING AT YOU.

"I'VE BEEN WORKING REAL HARD WITH THE DECORATOR," YOU SAY — JUST A JOKE, YOU CAN'T HELP IT — AND YOU WANT TO KICK YOURSELF BECAUSE THAT'S JUST THE KIND OF SARCASTIC COMMENT CRO MAGS HATE.

"HOW ABOUT A FEW MORE DUSTBALLS NEAR THE SOFA, FOR ATMOSPHERE?" BUD SUGGESTS.

AND YOU'RE AMAZED. A CRO MAG WITH A SENSE OF HUMOR!

JAY ROLLS UP HIS SLEEVES AND ASKS IF I HAVE KITCHEN TRASH BAGS.

SOON WE'VE STARTED. WE TOSS CLOTHES INTO BAGS. WE SWEEP.

We throw out food. We fix broken hinges. Bud opens windows you hadn't even realized were closed. We work, work, work.

And that's when you make your discovery: YOU ARE A RAVING, STEREOTYPING, PARANOID, IMMATURE fool, just as bad as the Cro Mags.

Because Bud is a good guy.

You actually have fun. By the end of the day, everyone's laughing at your jokes and asking you to do your imitations of Ms. Patterson and Mr. Dean.

And just before you go, Jay asks you if you want to go to his house Saturday. Just a "small hang with the guys," he calls it, and Lisa is rolling her eyes and teasing him for not inviting girls, so Jay has to make excuses and claim that he TRIED, but the other guys wouldn't let him — which makes you think this is really a Cro Mag gathering, but you don't want to ask right out, so you casually ask who'll be there, and Bud jumps in and mentions Sam and Travis and Marco — and you say you're not sure you can come, and Jay says, "I'll take care of Marco," so you think about it awhile.

Before today, you would have said you'd go to the party when hell freezes over.

But you realize that you were wrong about Bud.

Maybe you're wrong about some of the other guys.

Wouldn't it be nice to actually have them ON YOUR SIDE? To have so-called NORMAL guys as your friends?

You picture a new life. A house that can actually be a HOME, even without Mom & Dad. Guy friends your own age.

It COULD happen.

So you say yes.

The Morning After
In Homeroom

Ted is flabbergasted.

You know this because he came into your room this morning and woke you up, saying, "Ducky, I am flabbergasted."

You told him you'd be full of flabbergast too if your little brother had totally cleaned the house out of the goodness of his heart, without asking for so much as a dime.

Then he asked where his college jersey was, and why some of your socks ended up in his drawer, and whether or not you threw away his intro biology notes that were probably lying on the living room floor, etc., etc., and soon you felt like you'd done something terribly wrong.

But you didn't. You were actually able to open the fridge without worrying that something living would crawl out, and you could walk through the house to the front door without tripping over anything. THAT'S progress.

But that was nothing compared to what happened at school, when you saw Bud and Marco and Travis and a couple of other goons standing at the door in their familiar places.

Bud said hi.

Just HI.

No other singsongy voices or snickers or comments about your clothes or imitations of the way you walk — nothing.

So you said hi back.

And you strolled into school feeling about seven feet tall.

You could get used to this.

Today, friend of the Cro Mags. Tomorrow, who knows? Cigarettes, flannel shirts, and muttering with lots of one-syllable words.

Ha.

Ducky, you are SUCH a snob.

Anyway, at your locker, Jay was his usual self. Talking so fast you could barely understand him. He went on and on about Saturday, insisting it'll be fun, just hanging out, no big deal, etc. Then he asked a question you REALLY didn't expect.

Did you think ALEX wanted to come?

Alex? To a place where Cro Mags are invited? (To ANY party, for that matter?)

You burst out laughing. You told Jay he was nuts. You reminded him he hates Alex. You reminded him that all the Cro Mags hate Alex.

But Jay was totally serious. He said he's been getting on

THE CRO MAGS' CASES ABOUT THE INSULTS AND COMMENTS. HE'S CONVINCED THEM THAT ALEX AND YOU ARE GOOD GUYS, AND BUD HAS BACKED HIM UP. SO NOW THEY'VE PROMISED TO HAVE OPEN MINDS.

THEN JAY TOLD YOU THAT HE'S BEEN MISSING THE OLD DAYS LATELY. WHENEVER HE SEES ALEX AND YOU HANGING OUT, IT BRINGS BACK THE HAPPY TIMES YOU THREE SPENT TOGETHER. "MAYBE ALEX HAS GONE SLACKER ON US, BUT HEY, HE'S THE SAME GUY INSIDE, RIGHT?" JAY SAID. "ONCE A FRIEND, ALWAYS A FRIEND, THAT'S WHAT I SAY."

YOU COULDN'T ARGUE WITH THAT. SO YOU SAID YOU'D ASK ALEX IF HE WAS INTERESTED.

YOU'LL CATCH HIM AT LUNCH.

YOU KNOW THAT HE'S GOING TO SAY NO. BUT IT'S WORTH A TRY.

SOMETIMES —

RARELY, BUT SOMETIMES —

YOU'RE NOT AS SMART AS YOU THINK

YOU DID TELL ALEX ABOUT JAY'S GATHERING.

HE DIDN'T BELIEVE YOU.

WELL, HE DIDN'T BELIEVE JAY. HE THOUGHT THE INVITATION WAS A TRICK. BUT YOU TOLD HIM YOU WERE CONVINCED THAT JAY WAS JUST BEING FRIENDLY, JUST TRYING TO BRING BACK THE OLD TIMES, AND WHY NOT GIVE IT A TRY.

And then ALEX — Alex the Humor-Challenged — told a
joke.

He said that if Jay was trying to bring back the old times,
maybe we should show up with our Darth Vader masks and
plastic lightsabers, the way we used to when we were seven.

Not a GREAT joke, but a try. A good try. And it did
make you laugh, and you reminded him about the time we all
went trick-or-treating and Jay's bag grew much bigger than
ours and we didn't know why until we figured out that he was
stealing our candy while we weren't looking, and Alex
remembered some other crazy thing, and you were both
laughing so hard that you almost forgot to ask him again about
the "get-together."

But you did.
And he said yes.
And somehow you avoided fainting from shock.

Mirror, Mirror
On the Wall,
Who Are You Trying to Kid?

Ducky, you are nuts.
Take off the Penn State football jersey. You don't even

KNOW WHERE Penn State IS. Well, Pennsylvania, but that's not the point. Put it back where it belongs, in the closet with all the rest of the Christmas gifts from Uncle Chad, like the football and the metal bat and the '76ers autographed team poster.

YOU ARE NOT A CRO MAG.

YOU WILL NEVER BE A CRO MAG.

DON'T EVEN TRY TO LOOK LIKE ONE.

You should be ashamed of yourself.

In Which Ducky
Takes Hold of His Senses
And Prepares to Leave

I am nervous.

I am scared.

I am very, very, VERY glad that Alex is coming to this party.

I just called. He's ready and waiting for me to pick him up.

Here goes.

It'll be fine.

Lots of fun.

And if things get bad, we can always leave.

Late
Maybe Too Late

I don't know what to do — I'm home — alone — no, not alone — Alex is here too — but I might as well be alone because

What? What? My mind is jumping around and I'm forgetting things and I feel like I'm in shock or something, and it's so late I should be fast asleep but I can't sleep because I HAVE TO DO SOMETHING and besides, if I DO sleep what'll happen to Alex? And I WISH MOM AND DAD WERE HERE or at least Ted, Ted might know what to do, but it's so late now and I'm worried about HIM too, what if he's lying in the street somewhere and he has no I.D. and

Stop.

Get it together.

Alex is ASLEEP. BREATHING. Muttering to himself.

Let him be. Decide what to do AFTER he wakes up.

Think it over. Start from the top. You have time. Alex isn't going anywhere.

Okay.

The top.

7:30. This evening.

You pick up Alex. He's back to his old self. Not his OLD old self, as in happy Alex of long ago, but his NEW old self, as in quiet and gloomy. And you don't know what has caused this to

HAPPEN, SO YOU MAKE THE BEST OF IT, JOKING AROUND AND SINGING TO THE TAPE OF MAGGIE'S ROCK GROUP, VANISH, AND HAVE YOU EVER HEARD THEM AND YADA YADA YADA YOU'RE TALKING SO MUCH YOU SOUND LIKE JAY, AND ALEX IS JUST SITTING THERE LOOKING LIKE SOMETHING OUT OF A WAX MUSEUM.

FINALLY HE WARMS UP A LITTLE AND ASKS IF YOU "BROUGHT ANYTHING" TO JAY'S, AND YOU FIGURE HE MEANS A GIFT OR SOMETHING, SO YOU ASK IF IT'S JAY'S BIRTHDAY AND HE CRACKS UP, REALLY LAUGHS, AS IF YOU'VE JUST MADE A JOKE, AND YOU'RE SO RELIEVED HE'S COMING OUT OF HIS BAD MOOD THAT YOU LAUGH ALONG WITH HIM.

SO WE GET TO EUCLID AVE. AND JAY'S HOUSE. YOU SHUT OFF THE IGNITION AND LOOK AT ALEX, AND HE'S SMILING AND SUDDENLY YOU REMEMBER WHAT WE ALWAYS USED TO SAY TO EACH OTHER WHEN WE WERE KIDS — "MAY THE FORCE BE WITH YOU" — AND WHEN YOU SAY IT, HE LAUGHS AGAIN.

TWO LAUGHS IN ONE DAY. YOU HIGH-FIVE, LEAVE THE CAR, HEAD FOR THE PARTY. THE MUSIC IS SO LOUD, THE LAWN IS VIBRATING.

JAY GREETS YOU AT THE DOOR WITH A HOLLER THAT SOUNDS LIKE THE CALL OF A WILD BOAR — NOT THAT YOU KNOW THAT SOUND, BUT THAT'S THE GENERAL IDEA — AND HE PRACTICALLY PUSHES YOU AND ALEX INSIDE, SHOUTING ALL HIS "DUCKY-DUCKMAN-DUCKOMETER" VARIATIONS AND THEN SLAPPING ALEX ON THE BACK AND SAYING HOW HAPPY HE IS THAT THEY'RE BUDS AGAIN JUST LIKE THE OLD DAYS, AND ALEX IS SMILING AWAY NOW, BUT YOU'RE DISTRACTED BECAUSE somebody's shoving a bottle of beer at you, and you take it only because you don't want it to drop onto the Adamses' living room rug, which feels a little moist and squishy already.

And that's when you notice that the house — the neat Adams house that's always so perfect-looking, so full of expensive stuff that Mr. and Mrs. Adams loved to show off to Mom and Dad way back when you used to visit, so nice that you always felt awkward just walking in there, like you might bump into the cabinet full of delicate crystal or get mud prints on the Persian rugs — the house is SWARMING. Guys all over the place, shouting and laughing and smoking and drinking beer and eating chips and candy and pretzels, and two guys are leaning against the china cabinet and it's shaking, and you KNOW the Adamses would be having a coronary if they could somehow see what was going on.

And then, just like that, Alex is gone. He's not by the door, where you last saw him, but it's not easy to actually SEE anybody specifically, because it's pretty dark and smoky in the living room and everyone's moving around, jumping to the music — not exactly dancing, because no girls are there — and as you're scanning the place you notice that Marco is standing in the corner, staring right at you.

You sort of smile, sort of nod, and he comes walking toward you, puffing away on a cigarette, and saying, "Yo, Bambi, what are you drinking?" And you freeze up.

THIS is the new Cro Mag attitude?

THIS is the openmindedness?

Then it's as if Marco's reading your mind, because he starts laughing and says, "Yo, guy, just a joke, all right?" — and as he walks toward you, he is weaving, as if the house were a ship on stormy seas.

You try to laugh along. You watch Marco flick his cigarette ashes into a coffee cup at the edge of the piano top — only it's NOT a normal coffee cup, because you remember the collection it came from, the BONE CHINA collection that Mr. and Mrs. Adams used to brag about. And you notice that this expensive bone china cup is full of a liquid that is definitely NOT coffee, definitely STRONGER than coffee — and you realize that Jay will be in the DOGHOUSE if the cup breaks. So you pick it up, ashes and all, in front of Marco, and he laughs and says, "Oh, sorry to mess up your drink, har har!" so you pretend to laugh too, and you head toward the kitchen.

On the way, you pass by guys you don't know very well, guys you don't WANT to know, and a couple of guys you've never seen before.

Quickly you wash out the cup, dry it, and put it back in the china closet. And from behind you, someone reaches in and grabs a delicate little glass thimble from Mrs. Adams's collection, and she ALWAYS used to talk about how valuable

THAT IS TOO, SO YOU GRAB IT BACK, AND YOU REALIZE YOU'VE JUST TAKEN SOMETHING FROM MAD MOOSE MACHOVER.

YOU HAVE NEVER BEEN FACE-TO-FACE WITH MAD MOOSE. YOU HAVE NEVER WANTED TO BE. AND NOW THAT YOU ARE, YOU SEE YOUR LIFE PASS BEFORE YOUR EYES.

HE ACCUSES YOU OF STEALING HIS "SHOT GLASS." YOU EXPLAIN, "THAT'S MRS. ADAMS'S THIMBLE," AND IMMEDIATELY YOU CRINGE BECAUSE THE WORDS SOUND SO DORKY, AND SURE ENOUGH, MAD MOOSE THUNDERS, "SO WHAT, SWEETHEART?" AND REPEATS HIS CLEVER JOKE TO EVERYONE AROUND HIM, AND NOW YOU'RE STANDING THERE, WITH EVERYONE LAUGHING AT YOU, AND IT'S EVEN WORSE THAN SCHOOL BECAUSE THERE'S NO PLACE TO RUN TO, AND YOU REALIZE THAT JAY IS A TOTAL ROTTEN BETRAYING CREEP FOR INVITING YOU HERE, AND THAT YOU NEVER SHOULD HAVE EVEN THOUGHT OF COMING, AND YOU LOOK AROUND AGAIN FOR ALEX SO YOU CAN SPLIT.

AND THEN, OUT OF NOWHERE, JAY APPEARS. HE PUTS HIS ARM AROUND YOU AND TELLS MAD MOOSE, "IF YOU'RE GOING TO INSULT MY FRIEND, YOU'RE OUT OF HERE" — AND BUD'S WITH HIM TOO, BACKING HIM UP.

MY HEROES.

ANYWAY, MAD MOOSE MUMBLES SOMETHING AND WALKS AWAY. YOU'RE HAPPY TO ESCAPE WITH YOUR LIFE.

MEANWHILE, YOU'RE LOOKING AROUND FOR ALEX AGAIN AND HE'S NOWHERE, AND JAY IS ANNOUNCING STUFF TO BUD — OL' DUCKMEISTER AND I WERE LIKE BROS, WE DID EVERYTHING

TOGETHER, LIKE THE TIME WE BROKE THE BASEMENT WINDOW YADA YADA YADA . . .

And then, like a shot, Jay is off chasing Sam, who is heading out the back door with a large, expensive-looking liquor bottle.

You and Bud follow. The coolness of the night air feels great. The quietness does too, except that Jay's over by the garage, yelling at Sam for stealing his dad's scotch.

Another group of guys is sitting on the blacktop below the basketball hoop — and you notice that THEY have bottles too. And Jay starts yelling at them, but they're saying, hey, take it easy, we BROUGHT these, and it's only BEER, and besides, we're not IN your house, are we?

That's when you spot Alex again. He's alone, lurking in the shadows near the house.

You call his name, but he just walks inside without answering you.

You run in after him. You search the house. He's nowhere. Vanished.

You duck out the front. You see someone far down the street, walking away. You can't tell for sure that it's Alex, but you guess it is. You figure he's doing the smart thing, leaving.

Which YOU should do too, but you can't, because your car is wedged in by a double-parked Jeep Cherokee.

So you go inside to find out whose car it is, but you're too chicken to ask around, so you end up watching a horror movie on the VCR in the den, which only makes you tired and bored and wastes an hour and a half.

In retrospect, THIS was your big mistake.

After the movie you walk out of the den, and the first thing you see is that the living room is no longer a living room. It's a mosh pit. Guys are ramming into each other, hollering. Someone has moved the furniture off to the sides, but not the stuff ON it. So you run around the room, closing the piano top, putting Mrs. Adams's Steuben glass figurines in safer places — because SOMEONE'S GOING TO HAVE TO ANSWER FOR THIS.

Then you notice the liquor cabinet. It's open. Guys are pouring drinks, and Jay is nowhere in sight.

But Alex is. He's slumped in an armchair, a bottle in his hand, just staring at everyone with this weird smile.

You run over to him. You kneel down and talk. You ask if he's okay. He keeps saying, fine, fine, don't worry, everything's great. But he's slurring his words, and his eyes are red, and he seems to be in a whole other world.

And then someone JACKS UP THE MUSIC. You're right near the speakers, and you feel like someone is punching you in the ear.

You jump away. You run to turn it down.

And there's Jay, standing by the stereo, a beer in hand, SINGING ALONG!

You turn the volume down, and everyone starts screaming at you. You try to explain to Jay that Alex is in bad shape and you need to talk to him — but Jay doesn't even listen. He just says, "Lighten up, Duckman," and jacks the volume back up.

Louder.

Calmly you turn it back down, to medium-loud.

You are standing toe to toe with Jay now. In each other's faces. You smell the alcohol on his breath. He looks furious. You know he's NOT REALLY LIKE THIS. Deep inside, he's not an obnoxious Cro Mag. He's just a little drunk. But you're also losing patience. You suggest in a firm voice that maybe HE'S lightened up a little TOO MUCH.

Mistake. Jay slams his drink down on the stereo cabinet. He starts SPEWING. Loud. So everybody can hear: "That's it, Ducky, mess up my party! Make EVERYBODY mad! You can't change, can you? I think of ways to HELP you, I fix you up with BABES, I tell all these guys what a DUDE you are, I invite you to my party, I STICK UP FOR YOU against Mad Moose, who could probably kill me — and what do YOU do? What kind of friend are YOU? THIS is how you thank me?"

You try to speak. You try to calm him down. Fat chance.

Jay is practically spitting in your face: "I give you all these chances to be a NORMAL GUY, and what do you do? Act like a WIMP. Maybe that's the way you ARE, huh? Maybe there's a REASON you can't meet girls! Maybe I'm wasting my breath and all these guys are RIGHT about you —"

That does it. You see stars. You want to grab his bottle and hit him over the head.

You raise your fists.

Come on, Jay says.

FIGHT! yells the pack behind you.

You almost do it. You almost jump on him.

But you don't. You can't. Your eyes are filling with tears.

So you do the only thing you CAN do.

You LEAVE.

You don't care if the Jeep is still blocking your car. You'll drive onto the sidewalk if you have to.

Jay doesn't try to hold you back. As you walk through the living room, the volume shoots back up to ear-splitting.

You expect to see Alex still in the same chair, but he's not.

Part of you wants to go without him, but that wouldn't be right, so you go outside and walk around the house, looking. Then in through the back door again for a quick check inside, but you don't see him at all and you hate being here and you are LOSING PATIENCE with the amazing disappearing friend, so you decide to check upstairs and if he's not there, tough, you are GONE.

And that is where you finally see him. At the bathroom door. Struggling to turn the knob. In one hand he is holding the bottle of gin. It is almost empty.

You ask: Did you drink ALL of that?

Alex spins around, like you shocked him. He mutters something about having to go to the bathroom.

You can barely understand him. It's only been a few minutes since you last spoke to him, but he seems drunker.

You reach for the knob. It's a little tight, but you can turn it.

As you open the door, you explain that after he's done, you are driving him home.

He says nothing, goes inside, and slams the door behind him.

You listen for retching noises, but all you hear is running water. You sink to the carpet outside the door. No one else is upstairs. Now that you're alone, now that you can THINK and not feel like people are STARING at you and wondering how you could have been invited, you realize how tightly you are wound up. You want to cry, but you CANNOT give Jay the satisfaction of finding you in tears. You SHOULDN'T be here anyway, and you WOULDN'T be here if it weren't for Alex, if he weren't in such bad shape.

And you start to beat yourself up, because you know that YOU'RE the reason Alex is so drunk. If YOU hadn't insisted on taking him to the party, if YOU hadn't left him right at the beginning, if YOU hadn't gone off and watched a stupid grade-Z movie — if you hadn't NEGLECTED your friend WHO WAS DEPRESSED TO BEGIN WITH — none of this would have happened.

So you sit there, grinding your teeth, waiting and waiting as the water runs inside.

And then you notice something.

The running water is not the sound of a SINK.

It's louder. It's a SHOWER.

You knock. Everything okay? you ask.

Alex says yeah, fine.

So you sit back and wait.

The shower lasts a long time. Too long. In Alex's state, you realize he's liable to fall asleep standing up. And if he falls on the tiles, he could break a bone, hit his head...

You knock again.

No answer.

You call his name.

You yell his name.

Nothing.

You turn the doorknob.

It's locked.

Now you're panicked. You bang on the door with your fist. You push with your shoulder, but the door won't budge.

You need help. You need a key.

The last person IN THE WORLD you want to talk to is Jay, but you have to. You have no choice.

You race downstairs. Jay is in the kitchen, raiding his own refrigerator.

You grab him by the arm and tell him what happened.

For a moment a strange expression plays across his face, like he doesn't know what to do, yell at you, apologize, what?

But he catches on. He runs upstairs, and you follow close behind, asking WHERE HE KEEPS THE KEY.

WHAT KEY? HE ASKS. WHO EVER KNOWS WHERE THE BATHROOM KEY IS?

You get to the bathroom, and now you see a stain seeping under the door and onto the hallway carpet, growing in a dark semicircle.

Jay yells — OPEN THE DOOR, YOU'RE FLOODING THE BATHROOM — and bangs hard, but still all you can hear is the running water, splashing onto the floor tiles inside.

Together the two of you charge the door. Your shoulders hit with a loud thud.

You step back and try again.

The third time, the door cracks. The wood splits down the middle.

You kneel to charge again, but Jay stops you. He says if we break the door, we'll hurt ourselves. Instead, he steps back and gives the door a karate kick.

His shoe goes right through. So does half his leg. He yells in pain, and you kick like crazy, and soon a big chunk of the door gives way, and Jay pulls his leg out and you're able to reach in and turn the knob from the inside.

You push the door open and run in.

The air is thick with steam. The room smells faintly of alcohol. Alex's bottle is on the floor, floating in the bathwater that has spilled over the side of the tub.

The shower curtain is drawn shut.

You splash through the water and pull the curtain aside.

ALEX IS SPRAWLED OUT IN THE TUB, THE WATER ALMOST COVERING HIS FACE. HE IS FULLY CLOTHED.

AND UNCONSCIOUS.

YOU TURN OFF THE WATER. JAY IS REACHING INTO THE WATER, HOOKING HIS ARMS UNDER ALEX'S SHOULDERS. YOU GRAB ALEX'S FEET, AND THE TWO OF YOU PULL HIM OUT.

ALEX IS GROANING NOW, MOVING HIS HEAD FROM SIDE TO SIDE. YOU MANAGE TO SET HIM ON THE CLOSED TOILET, AND HE'S BLINKING AND LOOKING FROM YOU TO JAY. "WHAT ARE YOU DOING?" HE ASKS.

WHICH SEEMS LIKE THE STRANGEST QUESTION HE CAN ASK IN THIS SITUATION, SO YOU SAY THE ONLY THING YOU CAN: "WHAT ARE YOU DOING?"

JAY IS KNEELING BESIDE HIM, HIS ARM STILL TIGHTLY AROUND ALEX'S SHOULDER. YOU HAVE NEVER SEEN THE EXPRESSION THAT'S ON JAY'S FACE. HE LOOKS WILD-EYED, TOTALLY FREAKED OUT.

JAY'S VOICE IS PITCHED ABOUT AN OCTAVE HIGHER THAN NORMAL. WHAT ARE YOU, STUPID? HE YELLS. WHO SAID YOU COULD DO THIS? CAN'T YOU WAIT UNTIL YOU'RE HOME?

ALEX MUMBLES SOMETHING ABOUT GETTING DRUNK AND WANTING TO TAKE A SHOWER TO SOBER UP — BUT JAY KEEPS SCOLDING HIM, TELLING HIM AT LEAST HE COULD HAVE LEFT THE DRAIN OPEN LIKE A NORMAL PERSON — AND DESPITE THIS, JAY IS WIPING TEARS FROM HIS CHEEKS. OR MAYBE IT'S NOT TEARS. MAYBE IT'S THE HUMIDITY IN THE ROOM.

YOU'RE A BASKET CASE YOURSELF. YOU'RE IN TOTAL SHOCK. ALL YOU WANT TO DO IS GET ALEX OUT OF HERE.

You and Jay stand him up. Alex can barely walk, so you stand on either side of him and prop him up.

Slowly, carefully, you make your way to the landing and down the stairs. Alex is dripping water, and it's hard to hold onto him, but you manage to do it, across the living room and out the front door.

All around you, guys are yelling and cheering. "Way to go, ALEX!" shouts one. "First casualty of the night!" shouts another.

They have no clue. They think this is FUN.

You and Jay drag Alex across the lawn to your car. The double-parked Jeep, fortunately, is gone.

You dump Alex in the backseat. He tries to say something but immediately keels over and closes his eyes.

Jay mutters a few choice angry words, the nicest of which is JERK. But as you climb in and start the car, he says, "Take care of him. And call me, okay?"

You nod and drive off.

Your hands are a little shaky. Your shoes are wet and slippery on the accelerator. You have to concentrate like crazy just to drive, and you go REALLY slowly.

Your mind is racing. Where do you take him now — home? Out for a cup of coffee? Isn't coffee supposed to be good for drunkenness? Can you walk into a restaurant soaking wet?

You can't decide. You drive around the block. Then you drive in the direction of Las Palmas. You follow the edge of the park, just cruising, thinking.

And soon you hear sniffling from the backseat. You figure Alex is getting a cold, but that's not it.

He's crying.

You realize you are too. You ask if he's okay.

He says he's sorry for getting your car wet.

You tell him that's okay, the seats are vinyl, and worse has happened to them.

You look at him through the rearview mirror, but he's looking away. He's sobbing now, apologizing for being drunk and for using the shower. He keeps insisting that he only wanted to sober up, that's all — saying it over and over, as if you wouldn't believe him.

You keep reassuring him and soon you both fall silent. The cars whiz by outside, and you hear someone's car stereo booming away, and it all feels very eerie and uncomfortable, the two of you driving aimlessly, and you can't help feeling that Alex wants to say something but he's not saying it.

You ask him if he wants to go home, but he says no. So you decide to take him to your house.

By the time you arrive, Alex's face is bone-white. That's when he gets sick, in the flower bed by the side of the house.

As you lead him into the house, he is moaning, stumbling, making these dry clicking noises with his throat. You sit him down on the living room sofa and place an empty wastebasket nearby, just in case. Then you fetch some clothing from upstairs.

As he changes, he apologizes again and again — I shouldn't

HAVE DONE IT, I DIDN'T KNOW WHAT I WAS DOING, I WAS DRUNK, I DIDN'T MEAN IT — AND YOU CALM HIM DOWN, SHUSHING HIM, SAYING DON'T WORRY, NO ONE AT THE PARTY EVEN NOTICED, IT'S ONLY WATER, JUST TRY TO SLEEP, ETC.

The CLOCK CHIMES 11 AND YOU REALIZE MRS. SNYDER MUST BE FREAKING OUT. YOU MENTION THIS TO ALEX AND HE SAYS HE DOESN'T WANT TO GO HOME, SO YOU OFFER HIM A PLACE TO STAY FOR THE NIGHT IF HE CONTACTS HIS MOM AND LETS HER KNOW.

YOU BRING IN YOUR CORDLESS PHONE. HE CALLS HER AND SHE AGREES, BUT YOU NOTICE THAT WHILE HE'S TALKING TO HER, HIS VOICE IS QUIVERING — AND AFTER HE HANGS UP, HE STARTS SOBBING. WAILING. LIKE A LITTLE BOY.

DON'T EVER TELL ANYBODY WHAT HAPPENED TONIGHT, HE SAYS. PROMISE ME, DUCKY. IT HAS TO BE A SECRET. IT DOESN'T GO PAST YOU AND ME. AND TELL THAT TO JAY TOO.

SURE, SURE, I SAY.

SCOUT'S HONOR?

SCOUT'S HONOR.

AND THEN HE LOOKS AT YOU WITH THESE WET, WET EYES, AND TELLS YOU THAT YOU'RE THE ONLY PERSON HE CAN TALK TO ABOUT THIS STUFF. YOU'RE THE ONLY PERSON HE CAN TRUST. YOU AND DR. WELSCH — YOU TWO ARE LIKE EXTENSIONS OF HIMSELF, HE SAYS.

YOU DIDN'T REALIZE YOU MEANT THAT MUCH, SO NOW ALL OF THE THINGS YOU'VE DONE — SITTING WITH HIM AT LUNCH WHEN NO ONE ELSE WOULD, STOPPING TO TALK TO HIM AT THE BRIDGE IN LAS PALMAS,

STICKING WITH HIM THROUGH THIS WHOLE HORRIBLE EPISODE — ALL OF IT SEEMS WORTH IT, IN SOME STRANGE WAY.

HE'S LYING ON THE SOFA NOW, HIS VOICE SLURRING AND FADING, AND HE'S COMPLAINING ABOUT A HEADACHE, SO YOU GO GET SOME ASPIRIN, AND BY THE TIME YOU'RE BACK, HE'S FAST ASLEEP.

SO YOU SIT, WATCHING. LISTENING TO HIM BREATHE. TRYING TO FIGURE OUT WHAT ON EARTH JUST HAPPENED.

YOU HAVE HAD SOME WEIRD NIGHTS IN YOUR LIFE. DRIVING THE GIRLS HOME WHEN THE UPPERCLASSMEN TRASHED MS. KRUEGER'S HOUSE AND FRAMED THE 8TH-GRADERS. TRACKING DOWN SUNNY ON VENICE BEACH THE NIGHT SHE RAN AWAY FROM HOME.

THIS IS WEIRDER SOMEHOW.

YOU DON'T KNOW WHY, IT JUST IS.

SO YOU SIT AND WRITE.

AND HERE YOU ARE, STILL AT IT.

SCARED AND EXHAUSTED. WORRIED.

WHY DID HE DO THAT? WHY DID HE GET SO DRUNK? ALEX DOESN'T DRINK. AND WHY WOULD HE TAKE A SHOWER — WITH HIS CLOTHES ON — WITH THE DRAIN CLOSED?

HE WAS IN A HURRY? HE WAS TOO DRUNK TO KNOW WHAT HE WAS DOING? HE FLIPPED THE DRAIN SWITCH BY ACCIDENT?

WEIRD.

TOO WEIRD.

HAVE TO STOP THINKING ABOUT THIS.

HAVE TO STOP WRITING.

FATIGUED.

Need sleep.

Good n

It Is Two A.M.

Do You Know Where Your Sanity Is?

The drain.

It's down the drain.

It MUST be, to have the dream you just had.

You have switched places with Alex. You are inside him, at Jay's party. You're feeling depressed and you don't like anyone there, and everyone's drinking and it seems like a good thing to do, at least SOMETHING to do, so you grab a bottle and start swigging. And suddenly everything seems less loud, less obnoxious — just LESS — and you like the feeling for awhile until it takes you over, and now you're starting to feel worse and worse, because, like they tell you in school, alcohol is a DEPRESSANT and what could be worse for DEPRESSION than that? So you sink and sink, but you're already at rock bottom, so what happens?

You go below, you go under, you question why you're at the party, you question why you're even ALIVE, and what's worse, you desperately have to go to the bathroom, but the one downstairs is being used, so you trudge to the one upstairs, and

ALL YOU WANT TO DO IS RELIEVE YOURSELF, BUT YOU'RE IN THERE, AND THE LIGHTS ARE BRIGHT AND YOU SEE YOURSELF IN THE MIRROR — PASTY AND TIRED AND STRINGY-HAIRED AND SAD — AND YOU SEE THE SHOWER AND THE GLEAMING TUB AND YOU DECIDE THAT'S WHAT YOU NEED, SO YOU TURN ON THE WATER AND STEP IN BUT YOU'RE NOT THINKING, YOU'RE NOT SOBER ENOUGH TO TAKE YOUR CLOTHES OFF, AND THE NEXT THING YOU KNOW YOU'RE SITTING DOWN, TIRED AND SOOTHED BY THE WARMTH, AND YOU KNOW YOU'RE GOING TO FALL ASLEEP, SLIP DOWNWARD, DOWNWARD — AND YOUR HAND REACHES FOR THE DRAIN BECAUSE YOU WANT THE TUB TO FILL, BECAUSE MAYBE IF YOU SINK FAR ENOUGH, IF YOU SLEEP DEEP ENOUGH, YOU WON'T HAVE TO COME BACK.

IT'S A DREAM!

A NIGHTMARE.

IT'S CRAZY TO EVEN THINK THAT ALEX DID THAT.

YOU ARE WIRED, MCCRAE. YOU ARE CRAZED AND DISTURBED.

AND YOU WATCH TOO MANY HORROR FILMS.

FIRST OF ALL, EVEN IF ALEX HAD CONSIDERED WHAT YOU WERE DREAMING ABOUT, HE WOULD HAVE JUST RUN THE BATHWATER. WHAT'S THE POINT OF PUTTING THE SHOWER ON? BESIDES, HE COULDN'T EVEN TURN THE DOORKNOB WHEN YOU FIRST FOUND HIM. HOW COULD HE HAVE CLOSED THE DRAIN ON PURPOSE?

FORGET IT.

PUT IT OUT OF YOUR MIND.

Still.

Still, it doesn't hang together.

WHY did Alex say "What are you doing?" when he woke up in the bathroom? As if we were stopping him from DOING something?

Why was he SO UPSET? So ASHAMED? Apologizing SO MUCH? Insisting on keeping this all a secret?

It doesn't make sense.

I want to talk to him, but he's out like a light.

Okay. He couldn't have been THAT desperate. If he was, he would have told me.

He said I'm the only one he talks to.

Me and Dr. Welsch.

Dr. Welsch might know what's going on in Alex's mind.

He DEFINITELY should know about what happened tonight.

But I can't call him.

I TOLD Alex I'd keep his secret.

I promised.

He trusts me. He says I'm an EXTENSION of himself. I have to live up to that.

2:23

THOUGHT:
DR. WELSCH IS AN EXTENSION TOO.
SO TELLING HIM WOULD NOT BE BREAKING THE PROMISE.
WOULD IT?
THINK, McCRAE.
DO WHAT YOU HAVE TO DO.
DO
THE
RIGHT
THING

WHAT SEEMS LIKE
A LIFETIME LATER

DID YOU?
DID YOU DO THE RIGHT THING?
WHO KNOWS?
YOU'RE IN NO SHAPE TO DECIDE THAT NOW. IT'S STILL DARK OUT,
AND YOU CAN BARELY STAND UP, BUT YOU CAN'T SLEEP, YOU CAN'T
THINK OF SLEEPING YET. YOUR MIND IS SCREAMING AT YOU, YOUR
THOUGHTS ARE SLAMMING AGAINST THE SIDES OF YOUR BRAIN, AND YOU
HAVE TO FIND RELIEF SOMEHOW.

Now.

Here.

Write.

SEE what happened. Step by step.

You called Dr. Welsch on the kitchen phone. His answering machine picked up — WHAT DID YOU EXPECT? It was after two in the morning! — and you left a whispered message that probably didn't make much sense but you left your number and tried to make it clear that Alex needed help.

Then you went back into the living room, figuring Dr. Welsch would call in the morning, hoping the FACT that you called would calm you down, make you sleep better.

And you might have fallen asleep, it was hard to tell — but when the phone rang and you jumped out of the armchair to answer it, you noticed only ten minutes had passed.

You picked up before the second ring, and it was Dr. Welsch, sounding groggy but calm, very calm, just the opposite of you, tripping over your own words, trying to tell the whole story but making NO SENSE — and Dr. Welsch just took over the conversation, in a soft but businesslike way, asking specific questions: Where is Alex now? Is he physically hurt? Does he need a doctor?

The sound of his voice was soothing. Reassuring. You wanted to visit him YOURSELF, to lie on his couch and have a good cry and do whatever you do in a therapist's office. Your voice was choking up as you answered his questions, but you stuck with it,

AND SOON YOU WERE TELLING HIM ABOUT THE WHOLE NIGHT, STARTING FROM THE BEGINNING, FROM THE QUIET RIDE IN THE CAR, TO THE ARRIVAL AT THE PARTY, TO YOUR SEPARATION FROM ALEX, TO THE BOTTLE AND THE BATHROOM...

AND DR. WELSCH WAS SAYING, "MM-HM" AND "THAT MUST HAVE BEEN HARD FOR YOU," AND NOT MUCH ELSE, JUST LETTING YOU RAMBLE ON AND ON, UNTIL YOU CAME TO THE END AND YOU WERE IN TEARS, SPEAKING AND SOBBING AT THE SAME TIME, ASKING FOR ADVICE — WHICH DR. WELSCH GAVE, TELLING YOU NOT TO WORRY, THAT ALEX WAS GOING TO BE ALL RIGHT, AND YOU WERE A GOOD FRIEND FOR CALLING, AND YOU WERE DOING THE RIGHT THING TO LET HIM SLEEP COMFORTABLY, BUT YOU HAD TO MAKE SURE THAT ALEX CAME TO SEE HIM FIRST THING TOMORROW.

YOU FELT MUCH BETTER AFTER YOU HUNG UP. BUT THE FEELING DIDN'T LAST LONG.

BECAUSE YOU TURNED TO SEE ALEX STANDING BEHIND YOU. LEANING AGAINST THE KITCHEN DOORWAY.

YOU PRACTICALLY JUMPED OUT OF YOUR SEAT IN SURPRISE.

ALEX HAD THIS TIGHT, BLANK EXPRESSION ON HIS FACE. FOR A MOMENT, YOU THOUGHT HE WAS GOING TO THROW UP AGAIN.

BUT HE DIDN'T.

HE SPOKE. HIS VOICE WAS CHOKED AND RASPY. AND VERY, VERY ANGRY.

HE CALLED YOU A TRAITOR.

HE SAID HE THOUGHT HE COULD TRUST YOU, BUT HE WAS WRONG.

You tried to explain. You told him you were worried. You said you'd dreamed that he'd tried to kill himself.

So you called Welsch because of a dream? Alex spat out.

Well, DID you try to kill yourself? you asked.

But Alex didn't answer. You know he heard you, but he ignored the question. You PROMISED, he said. Is that what a PROMISE means to you?

You reminded him about what HE'D said — about you and Dr. Welsch being extensions — but as the words came out of your mouth, they sounded so hollow, like an EXCUSE, like a kid saying nyah-nyah-nyah-nyah-nyah.

Alex just let those words hang in the air, his face twisting with disgust.

That's it, Ducky, he said. The friendship is over.

And he stomped away, toward the front door.

You ran after him. Asked where he was going. Told him to stay. Reminded him IT WAS LATE and MANIACS were out on the street at this hour and he couldn't possibly WALK all the way home — but he was acting like you weren't there, just walking away and not looking over his shoulder, right through your front door.

So what can you do when your former friend walks out into the streets of Palo City at 3 A.M. and you have NO IDEA what he's going to do, because everything he HAS done so far that day has been totally UNPREDICTABLE, and you

KNOW THAT IF SOMETHING HAPPENED TO HIM, YOU COULD NEVER FORGIVE YOURSELF?

You FOLLOW HIM.

You GET INTO YOUR CAR AND TAIL HIM THROUGH THE NEIGHBORHOOD. You ROLL DOWN YOUR WINDOW AND CALL OUT TO HIM, OFFERING HIM A RIDE.

AND EVEN THOUGH HE SAYS NASTY THINGS TO YOU AND TELLS YOU TO GO AWAY, EVEN THOUGH HE DUCKS INTO ALLEYWAYS AND BEHIND STRANGERS' HOUSES AND THROUGH EMPTY LOTS, YOU STAY WITH HIM AND YOU DON'T LET HIM OUT OF YOUR SIGHT.

AND SOON HE GIVES UP AND WALKS DOWN THE MIDDLE OF THE STREET, PRETENDING YOU'RE NOT THERE. AND YOU FEEL RELIEVED WHEN HE ENDS UP AT HIS HOUSE, AND ALL THE LIGHTS ARE OUT, WHICH MEANS HIS MOM HAS GONE BACK TO SLEEP AND WON'T MAKE A BIG SCENE.

AND YOU DON'T LEAVE, EVEN THEN, BECAUSE IN ALEX'S STATE OF MIND HE CAN DO ANYTHING. HE CAN WAIT FOR YOU TO GO AND THEN SNEAK OUT AGAIN — YOU DON'T EVEN WANT TO IMAGINE WHAT ELSE HE COULD DO — SO YOU PARK HALFWAY DOWN THE BLOCK, JUST BEYOND SIGHT OF THE HOUSE, AND YOU WALK BACK ALONG THE SIDEWALK, HIDING BEHIND THE TALL JUNIPER TREES NEXT DOOR.

You SQUAT THERE, LOOKING AT ALEX'S HOUSE. You SEE THE LIGHT GO ON IN THE DOWNSTAIRS BATHROOM, YOU HEAR THE SHOWER, AND YOUR HEART STARTS TO RACE. You SCAN THE HOUSE FOR A WAY TO SNEAK IN — JUST IN CASE — BUT THERE'S AN "INSTANT ARMED RESPONSE" SIGN IN THE FRONT WINDOW, WHICH WILL SET OFF AN ALARM IN SOME

POLICE STATION. WHICH, WHEN YOU THINK ABOUT IT, MIGHT BE A USEFUL THING — THE "INSTANT" AND "RESPONSE" PARTS — JUST IN CASE.

THE SHOWER RUNS ON AND ON, AND IT'S DRIVING YOU CRAZY, AND YOU START LOOKING FOR A ROCK TO THROW IN THE WINDOW —

THEN THE WATER NOISE STOPS.

YOU FREEZE.

A FEW MOMENTS LATER, THE BATHROOM LIGHT GOES OUT.

THEN ANOTHER LIGHT FLICKS ON. ALEX'S BEDROOM.

YOU SEE THE SILHOUETTE OF ALEX'S HEAD BRIEFLY, AND THEN THE SHADES ROLL DOWN.

YOU DO NOT MOVE. EVEN AFTER THE LIGHT GOES OUT, YOU STAY THERE. RIVETED. EYES SCANNING THE HOUSE. EARS LISTENING FOR ODD NOISES.

YOU STAY THERE — HOW LONG? IT FEELS LIKE HOURS, BUT YOU'RE NOT WATCHING THE CLOCK — AND FINALLY YOU'RE READY TO DROP FROM FATIGUE AND YOU DON'T WANT TO BE FOUND TOMORROW MORNING SLEEPING UNDER THE NEIGHBOR'S JUNIPER, SO YOU STAND UP AND STUMBLE ON CREAKY LEGS TO YOUR CAR.

AND ON THE WAY HOME, QUESTIONS NAG YOU LIKE MOSQUITOES.

DID YOU DO THE RIGHT THING?

DID YOU DO ALL YOU COULD?

DID YOU HELP ALEX?

AND MOST IMPORTANT, WHAT NEXT?

WHILE I WAS AWAY, TED CAME HOME. HE'S SNORING PEACEFULLY IN HIS ROOM. AT LEAST THAT'S ONE PERSON I DON'T HAVE TO WORRY ABOUT.

He's lucky. His life is simple.

I wish I felt tired. It's almost morning and I HAVE to sleep. Tomorrow could be big.

I KNOW why I can't sleep. I'm afraid of the morning. I have to do SOMETHING, but what? Call Alex? Talk to his mom? Call Dr. Welsch to see if Alex talked to him? Go over to his house and DRIVE him over to Dr. Welsch?

What if Alex denies what happened? What if he doesn't remember?

And what about Jay? He's going to want to know how Alex is. Do I tell him? Should I bring him into this?

Maybe Alex needs his friends to rally around him. Or maybe he needs to be left alone.

Am I doing enough?

Am I doing too much?

Where exactly do I fit into all this?

I don't know.

That's the problem.

I SHOULD know, but I don't.

I'm sitting here at 4:30 in the morning, so awake I could run a marathon, writing my brains out because I can't TALK to anybody — considering I've already broken a vow of silence, and Ted would be useless about stuff like this even if I COULD tell him, and Mom and Dad don't like me to call Ghana — so all I CAN do is write, and that should be helping me, because PUTTING IT ON PAPER always makes thoughts clearer, and I've

FILLED UP A WHOLE JOURNAL, WEARING OUT MY FINGERS, EXAMINING EVERY POSSIBILITY, DISSECTING, REASONING, SPILLING. AND AFTER ALL THAT, I SHOULD HAVE AN IDEA, I SHOULD KNOW WHAT PATH TO TAKE, I SHOULD HAVE AN UNDERSTANDING AT LEAST, AND MAYBE A STRATEGY.

I'M NOT A STUPID GUY. I SHOULD HAVE ALL OF THAT.

BUT I DON'T.

I REALLY DON'T KNOW WHAT TO DO.

EXCEPT WORRY.

AND HOPE.

L. GODWIN

Ann M. Martin

About the Author

ANN MATTHEWS MARTIN was born on August 12, 1955. She grew up in Princeton, NJ, with her parents and her younger sister, Jane.

Although Ann used to be a teacher and then an editor of children's books, she's now a full-time writer. She gets the ideas for her books from many different places. Some are based on personal experiences. Others are based on childhood memories and feelings. Many are written about contemporary problems or events.

All of Ann's characters are made up. But some of her characters are based on real people. Sometimes Ann names her characters after people she knows, other times she chooses names she likes.

In addition to California Diaries, Ann Martin has writen many other books, including the Baby-sitters Club series. She has written twelve novels for young people, including *Missing Since Monday*, *With You or Without You*, *Slam Book*, and *Just a Summer Romance*.

Ann M. Martin does not live in California, though she does visit frequently. She lives in New York with her cats, Gussie and Woody. Her hobbies are reading, sewing, and needlework—especially making clothes for children.

Look for #6

SUNNY

4:10 P.M.

WHY WHY WHY DO I HATE BEING HERE SO MUCH?

WHY DO I FEEL SICK?

WHY DO I FEEL LIKE I'M GOING TO FAINT?

I'VE BEEN HERE A MILLION TIMES. I SHOULD BE USED TO IT BY NOW.

I AM VISITING MOM.

I AM HER DAUGHTER.

I SHOULD BE LOVING AND SUPPORTIVE AND INTERESTED AND SYMPATHETIC

AND ALL I CAN THINK OF IS GETTING OUT OF HERE.

I KNOW WHY.

IT'S DAWN.

I SHOULD NEVER HAVE COME WITH HER.

DAWN THE DEVOTED. DAWN THE PERFECT AND
PERKY.

How. CAN. SHE. BE. So. UP?

"HI, MRS. WINSLOW. YOU'RE LOOKING SO PRETTY,
MRS. WINSLOW. IS THERE ANYTHING I CAN DO FOR
YOU, MRS. WINSLOW? COME ON, SUNNY, LET'S PROP
UP THE BED/CALL THE NURSE/GET YOUR MOM SOME
FOOD/TELL HER ABOUT SCHOOL TODAY."

AND NOW SHE'S IN THE BATHROOM, HELPING
MOM, WHILE I'M OUT HERE FEELING LIKE A JERK.

I SHOULD BE WITH MOM. I WOULD BE TOO IF
MY BEST FRIEND WEREN'T SUCH A GIRL SCOUT.

I WANT TO HELP. BUT WHENEVER I'M ABOUT TO
OFFER IT, DAWN SPEAKS UP FIRST.

WHEN THAT UGLY NURSE CAME IN AND THOUGHT
DAWN WAS MOM'S DAUGHTER, I WANTED TO SCREAM.